MY FEMDOM MARRIAGE VOL. 2

The Princess of a Dozen Slaves

PhDomme Emma
Edited by: Daniel Sullivan

The University of Slavery and Servitude

CONTENTS

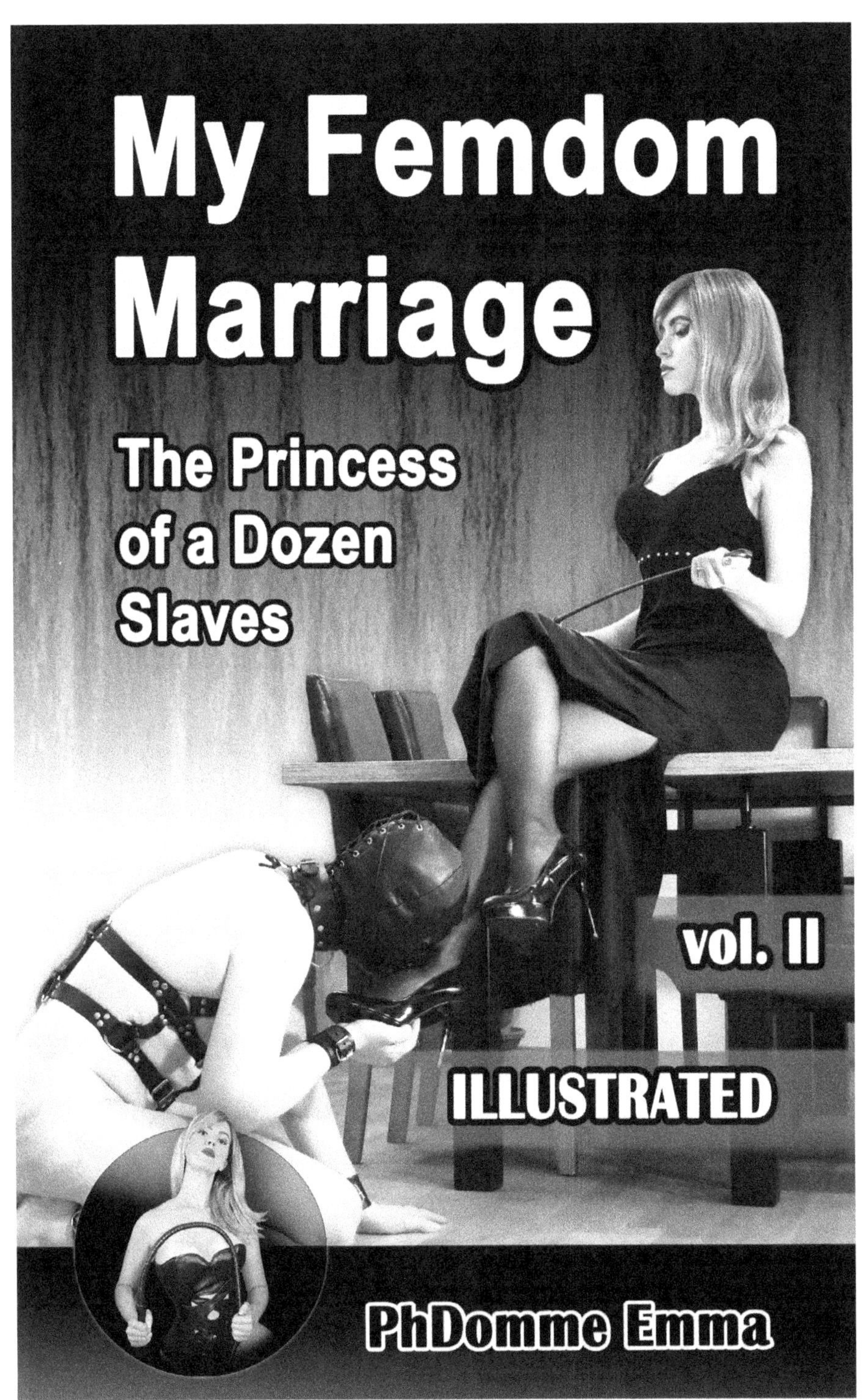
My Femdom
Marriage
The Princess
of a Dozen
Slaves
vol. II
ILLUSTRATED
PhDomme Emma

Find The Uncensored Images For This Book At:

https://universityofslavery.com/galleries/

CHAPTER 1

2016

Tom arrived home, closed the door of the flat and breathed a relieved sigh. The idea of leaving the mad world outside and again dropping to his knees in front of his Goddess was comforting beyond anything. He expected she was there and he could hardly wait to greet her. His wife's alter ego, Mistress Rebecca, was surely getting ready to meet him in her high stilettos and figure hugging pencil skirt, just like on most working days.

He walked past a reproduction of Brancusi's Princess X and in the hall, carelessly threw his keys into the bowl. Their spacious loft on the block of flats was designed to reflect the passion for abstract art that he and his wife shared. He noticed her keys weren't there, but he wasn't concerned. She often dropped her keys in her handbag. Tom checked himself in the mirror next to the entrance door. He looked dead tired. It was no wonder too, as he had spent hours at an exhausting meeting. Before he could enter the bathroom to freshen up his weary face, something unusual met his eye.

The large, full-length mirror in the hallway was covered with red scribble. Tom stopped in his tracks and turned to face it. He was rather short-sighted and squinted on the ornate scripture. Finally he made out the message, reading out loud:

Hi there,

No, I'm not at home.

Time to draw you out of your routine!

Meet me in the Playce at seven.

Wear the pink one!

R.

Tom stared in bewilderment. He and his wife planned to have an exciting Femdom evening and she wanted to meet him in a shopping mall instead? For a moment he mused, why his wife of two years decided to cover the mirror with lipstick instead of sending a text like an ordinary wife would. But he answered himself - Rebecca is by no standards an ordinary wife. She always was a force of nature, but ever since she entered the Dominant Wives' Club, she was surpassing all he ever hoped she might become, for good and bad. Long gone were his couch potato days. Rebecca was an exacting, demanding and pretty stern Mistress.

Sometimes he remembered with nostalgia the days gone by, when he used to drink beer and watch football, chill with video games, or go to the pub with his friends. Overall though, he felt more fulfilled and happy than he had ever felt. The influence of her friends Mistress Emma, Mistress Cruella and other Ladies of the Club in this sudden transformation was undeniable.

He strained his brain to make out, what was 'the pink one' she referenced. Sometimes he was rather slow at catching a hint... He noticed a symbol of a stiletto shoe below the scribble. This was their secret code for Femdom that found its way into their texting communication and was used whenever secrecy was advised. It suddenly dawned on him and he slapped his forehead. The new chastity device his Mistress got for his maid training!

Tom woke at once from the temporary stupor when he checked his watch. If he was to meet her at the shopping mall, he had just twenty minutes. His hands unconsciously sought his crotch. The elastic milky white tube his Mistress used to give him spankings on his penis, sprang up in his mind. She was so fond of chastising him for late arrivals... each minute equaled one stroke. His penis was violet most of the time. He was the renowned latecomer at family gatherings and hardly ever made it to work on time. He was horrified by the prospect of getting another beating on his already sore member... Now he had to press it through the ring and snap on the cage in shortest time he ever managed.

In lightning speed Tom jumped into the shower, almost killed himself on the slippery tiles and ripped the bathroom curtain in the process. Clumsily, he slipped on the pink cage, grateful that this time it didn't take him a solid ten minutes to get his joy department through the ring. With mismatched socks and a streaming shirt he flew through the door, shutting it with a bang. He loudly stormed down the stairs and jumped into the car, hastily buttoning the shirt as he went. The key to his chastity device he dropped into his chest pocket. His phone pinged - the unmistakable bubble sound reserved solely for the messages from his Mistress.

"I hope you are on your way, my hand is beginning to itch." A message, with the unmistakable shoe symbol! She meant business...

Tom drummed his fingers on the wheel as he got stuck in the traffic and willed the universe to slow down, together with his Tissot wristwatch. By a lucky coincidence, traffic was not as insane as other days. Finally, he was arriving to the Potsdamer Platz and dived into the garage, his tires screeching on the rubbery surface and leaving dark marks and stench of burnt rubber. Another short message arrived.

It read. "... Dress for success. Where girls go to look sexy?"

Tom broke out in a cold sweat. He was running out of time and couldn't afford to fumble in the dark. He had to get it right the first time, if he was to avoid the dreaded beating. He looked at his watch. He was already late two minutes. Damn. The more he taxed his tired brain, the less focus he was able to squeeze out of it.

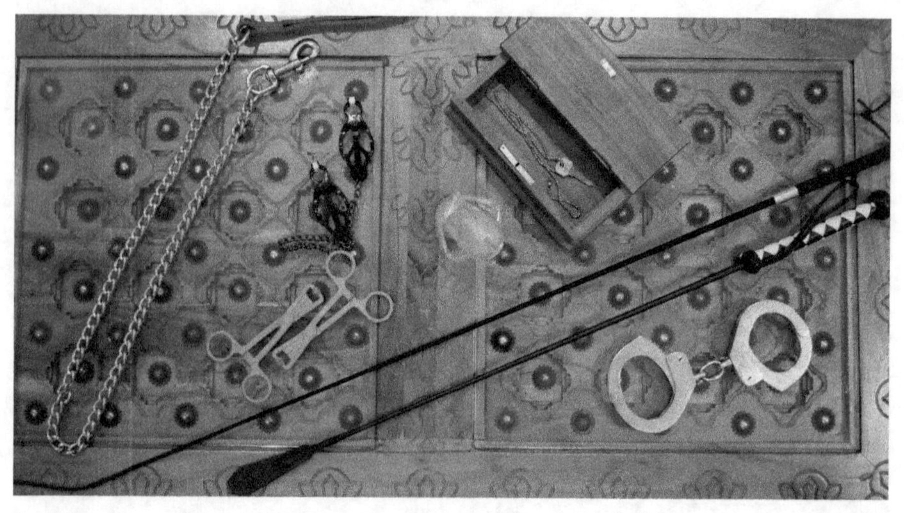

CHAPTER 2

2007

A tall blonde in a luxury grey fur was briskly walking on the pavement, adjacent to a city park. As usual in the early autumn evening, it was completely dark. It was also raining and the woman in high boots walked swiftly, her step betraying she was aware that it isn't a safe place to be after the sunset. As she was walking, she scanned the surrounding dark shrubs with her eyes for any signs of potential trouble. On the road, cars were whooshing around. She walked as close to the forest as possible, wary of getting struck by the mud when the cars hit the puddles of rain water.

One car turned to enter the side street, running along the main road. The dark red Volkswagen slowed down, copying her speed.

She noticed it, but pretended not to.

She looked around and recognized a billboard. This was it - the hallmark he talked about. It was shining in the dark and said: In 2007, vote number 7! The picture on the sign showed a porky, red faced man, whose ambition to be the next city mayor was written all over his greasy face, smiling at her with his crooked teeth. Even though there were other things on her mind, she thought that the guy stood no chance against his handsome opponent whose flashy smile beamed from another billboard across the street.

At the crossroads, she turned left. The lamp at the entry to the city park was out of order. To the passers-by it would look like she was swallowed by the darkness. The car that seemed to pursue her, parked in close vicinity. She gave it a last wide-eyed look and disappeared into the forest.

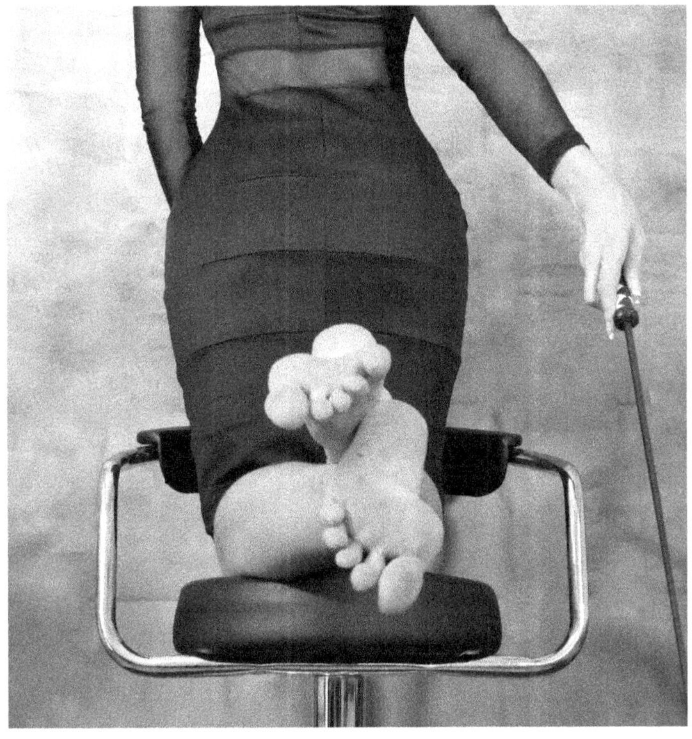

CHAPTER 3

2016

Tom sprinted up the stairs to the first floor, not caring who he knocked over in the process. Breathing heavily and clutching his side, he arrived in front of a luxuriously decorated shop window of a posh lingerie boutique. Rebecca was already inside - he could see her joking with the shop assistants. Tom breathed a heavy sigh of relief. His body was sending pain signals to his side, indignant at this abrupt and completely unsolicited exercise. He bet on the right card and here he was, almost boasting with pride that he solved the riddle. The elevated feeling was giving way to unease - he was five minutes late. He hoped against hope she would not notice.

Rebecca spotted him and turned around to meet him, sending

her hair flying.

"Oh, there he is... my sweet little hubby! Pray come in," Rebecca sang in an innocent voice. She might have deceived the shop keepers, but he knew just by the sound of her voice that his wife had some devilish scheme up her sleeve. She stretched both hands out to him and with a bright smile she welcomed him. Hesitating, he took her perfectly manicured little hands and allowed himself to be pulled into the shop. She looked glorious of course.

Ever since she became a Domme, her confidence was radiating from her every gesture and she took even greater care of her looks. The crystals, weaved into long curtains in the shop window could not outshine her. Two pretty young shop assistants with smooth buns wore perfectly unnatural professional smiles and cordially greeted him.

"Dear, I cannot decide which of these suits me better, will you please help me with that?" she said in a theatrically helpless tone and waved a selection of sexy, audaciously overpriced underwear.

Before he could say a word, Tom was ushered into a fitting room. Rebecca drew the curtain with a devilish grin. She pressed the hangers against his chest. Tom grabbed it, awkwardly staring at his wife. "Are you going to try these on?"
She didn't respond and smirked. She folded her arms in front of her, waiting for him to connect the dots with a condescending smile. The longer it took him, the more amused and sarcastic she looked.

Finally it dawned on him and his mouth popped open. "Surely you don't mean?" He whispered, his eyes wide open with horror.

"Honestly, darling, sometimes I'm a little worried if some bug did not eat the parts of your brain responsible for reading clues and guessing riddles."

He pulled his arms closer to himself like a shy virgin. "You want me to put it on... like, right here?" His eyes shot unconsciously sideways, through the curtains, where he sensed the shop assistants. They could at any moment drop by and ask how the lingerie fit... In a boutique like that the employees were royally overpaid to be obliging and attentive. Needless to say, their attention often balanced on the verge of nosiness.

Rebecca glided her palm down his chest... way down to his trousers. She grabbed his crotch, while with her other hand she stole into his chest pocket and took possession of the tiny key.

"Yes, Fuckboy, right here, right now!"

With an air of a Hollywood star Rebecca dropped the key into her bra and with both hands fixed her boobs. He watched her self-assured ways and was smitten. She was playing the secret chords of his carefully guarded fantasies. Even now, a whole year after she dived into Femdom, he still was shocked with moments of wonder and awe. He never before dreamed that one day she would share with him his kinks, and not only share them, but take charge and guide the way to their exploration.

She unzipped his trousers and rolled down his underwear, exposing the pink chastity cage.

"It looks even better than I hoped! But don't think for a second that it will spare you the punishment for your late arrival." She got hold of his cock and balls, fitted in the pink plastic. She pulled on it slightly, toying with the balls that, pressed through the ring, were hard and smooth. She leaned closer and her tresses tickled him on the cheek. She smelled divine, it was the Versace perfume he learned to associate with her dominant role.

Just the smell alone was making him horny.

"Today starts a new era! You won't be just the Fuckboy anymore, you are getting a brand new identity! Tomorrow evening you will transform into Priscilla, my new house maid. But first, we need to select some pretty underwear for her. You see, my female servant can't walk around without proper attire! I want to enjoy what I see, when I fuck her up her ass. Let's see what will fit the best!"

Ambivalent emotions were whirling in his mind. For one, he was mortified by the idea of the shop assistants seeing him wearing a black bodice laced with pink in the front and with an opening in the crotch where his matching pink cage was peeping through the cut out. On the other hand he was getting pleasantly thrilled by Rebecca's dirty talk. In the last months she was coming up with cross dressing ideas and humiliating games more and more often to push the limits of his submission.

Rebecca pointed imperiously to the tip of her high boots and hissed: "Now kiss, Fuckboy." He eagerly obeyed, blood at once hurling into his head as he dived down and covered her shoes with kisses. The curtain wasn't reaching to the floor, it was few inches shorter. He could see the legs of customers and assistants as he was kissing Rebecca's shoes. This did not ease his mind.

"Now you will put on this sexy female underwear." Tom hesitated, but he knew that Rebecca was pretty determined to make him obey. He could hear melodious voices of the shop assistants, mingling with the lounge music, but he couldn't make out the words due to the hubbub from the large shopping mall. They seemed to be busy arranging the goods and selling to other customers. Hopefully, they wouldn't come check. He took a deep breath and opened his trousers and rolled them down to his ankles.

CHAPTER 4

2016

The company Tom worked for was in the middle of a crisis. Their biggest competitor introduced a groundbreaking new technology that rendered their old-fashioned production of plastic parts obsolete. As a production director, he was supposed to come up with a brilliant new idea about how to keep their business afloat. At the moment, however, he wasn't coming up with any ideas at all. Try as he might, every time he willed himself to focus on the dull columns of numbers, the events of yesterday's evening sprang up on his mind.

He twirled a pen, his gaze absentmindedly fixed on a scruffy guy, who was washing the glass facade on the outside of their office building. Blood was traveling to his crotch and making his trousers tight. Tom didn't wear a chastity cage at work anymore - ever since a lunatic stole into their company with a knife, all employees had to pass through a metal detector. As he found out (to his great embarrassment at the airport few weeks ago), even the plastic cage could set off the alarm with its metal lock.

But Rebecca had just the other day made him order plastic wire tabs with unique numbers that acted as non-metal locks to secure his chastity cage in place. The metal detectors would not pose a problem any longer. Devilish Rebecca made a point of taunting him that as her chastity slave, he had no name and would be referred to by using the unique number on his plastic lock, such as slave #78567.

The day before Rebecca dragged him into the fitting room and mercilessly insisted he try on all the ridiculously tiny thongs and bras, and the notion of being seen by the shop assistants was pretty terrifying. But now he felt a rush of excitement when he thought about it. Some situations and phrases were running like a loop in his brain. He vividly recalled Rebecca saying: "Wait for the expression of the Ladies of the Club, when they see you En Femme and serving me!"

This idea kept coming back like a boomerang. He could see the pretty Mistress Valeria, the impishly grinning Mistress Cruella and first and foremost, the young Goddess Eva, the prettiest and youngest of all. He sensed that Rebecca was not just teasing him. Not this time. She was bringing up the subject of maid service and slutty maids so often, it couldn't be a coincidence. He could tell she was determined to put him in that role and he feared it was coming soon.

When they got home, Rebecca whipped his cock with the elastic tube for his late arrival. The adrenaline rush they both experienced during the boutique visit was transformed into the energy of pure kink. Rebecca insisted on him putting on the underwear they purchased. Tom could still see the curious look at the shop assistant's face when they walked out of the fitting room and he was carrying the selected goods. Did she have any suspicion? She might have seen his bare feet under the curtain... She might even have noticed he was trying on the stockings. But all these worries soon made way to the thrilling scene Rebecca played out.

When Rebecca commanded, Tom happily embarked on the journey to become the house maid she desired, even though he was rather apprehensive about the new course of their Femdom relationship. Of course he knew this idea did not originate in her own head. The Ladies of the Club undoubtedly were behind this - they knew him and his most secret desires better than anyone. Their insight into his submissive mind was unparalleled and came down to the depth of their experience. They sensed it - way down, under the layers of his psyche, deep down below his kinks and fetishes lay his suppressed desire to be feminized, humiliated and raped like a slut.

The previous night in his dreams Tom lived through the situation all over again. His sleeping mind conjured up what the waking world would shy away from. The Rebecca of his dream was glamour itself - a dangerous amazon in shiny boots, with seven inch ruby red nails. She played him like a violin and he was yielding to her every touch. She dressed him completely in the ladies' underwear - a super-tight translucent bodice with feathery lining, complete with garters and stockings. When he was ready, she looked him deeply in the eye. "You look far too good, my sissy, to stay hidden from the world."

In the dream he looked at himself in the mirror - to his utter surprise, he was wearing slutty make up with false lashes and bright red lipstick, his nails covered with glittery polish. Rebecca placed a blond curly wig on his head and pulled it down on the temples for better fit. Not minding his protests, she snapped a pink lead to the ring on his lace-lined collar and pulled him out of the fitting room. He looked down on his body and could see his cage crammed pathetically against the figure-hugging fabric.

"What? You got a sissy here? You should have said, I like to have fun humiliating them," one of the shop assistants chirped. Rebecca just smiled and invited the two girls to join her. Rebecca and the shop assistants humiliated him in front of the flabbergasted customers, who just froze with their hands holding the lingerie to gape at the show. The women made him sniff their feet and laughed at his tiny cock in the pink cage, calling it 'clitty'. They were abusing him verbally by saying what a good slut he would make and that he would be exhibited to all the pretty women shopping around in the shopping mall. Suddenly, all the members of the Club materialized out of thin air. They pointed, whispered and laughed to his pathetic appearance.

Mistress Eva, who wore astonishingly high boots with real spurs, said: "Wait till you meet my very well-endowed boyfriend, Helmut. He is horny all the time, I hardly keep up. My pussy needs some rest. You will quench his desire instead of me! A slut like you is good for only one thing - getting banged morning, noon and night! Look, here he comes!"

Tom, horrified, jerked his head to look in the direction Princess Eva pointed, but at that precise moment last night he remembered waking up. Drowning in the dark, he realized his body was clammy and his sheets cold and wet. He sweated profusely throughout his wild dreams and woke with a massive erection.

"Ehm..." a small voice sounded right next to Tom. He gave a start upon waking up from this daydream repeat. "Sir? Did you hear me?" It was his assistant, a lad of nineteen with coarse orange hair and freckles.

"Um, sorry, Gordon, what did you say?" Tom fidgeted in his chair, fortunately his erection was gone before he rose to solve whatever it was that needed solving.

"A man is waiting for you in the lobby," the assistant informed. Tom scratched his head. Did he forget about something? He briefly checked his calendar. No business meeting that day. Before he could ask about particulars, his assistant was gone, loudly talking on the phone.

Tom, confused, walked into the lobby. A scrawny guy with a mane of curly hair, dressed in an awkward combination of baggy pants and elastic leggings was erratically pacing the lobby. "Yes?" Tom said.

The guy, who abruptly stopped, grimaced an impatient face. "Please take this already, I have like a gazillion commissions after you."

Tom hesitantly took the box the messenger was handing to him. "What is it?" he asked.

"How am I to know?" the guy said, as if Tom was the stupidest creature he ever had to lay his eyes on. "Just take it, will you? Your signature - here. Thanks. Bye!"

Tom took the box and returned to his office. What could it be? Suddenly, his phone pinged.

"You want to open this in private." It was from Rebecca. Ahhh... of course. Another of her surprises! She cannot just give whatever it is to him at home, she needs to send a messenger. He stealthily looked around to see, if he was being watched. Then he realized that the only suspicious thing is his own behavior, so he composed himself and waited for his colleagues to go to lunch.

CHAPTER 5

2007

A man with deep eye sockets and a bald, tattooed head appeared on the park pavement, just as if he materialized out of thin air, as if he was a moth attracted by the yellow light of the park lamp.

"There you are." He approached the brunette in the grey fur soundlessly and gave her a start. "That's very nice fur," he said, and touched the sleeve. It felt improper and intrusive, but she resisted the temptation to slap his hand - something she would surely do in other circumstances. "Is it chinchilla? It is so soft... I always thought that their fur is like touching a soft breeze." He was eying her insolently, scanning her head to toe, standing too close to her, invading her personal space.

"Yes, it is a pleasure to meet you too," she replied in a tone that made quite clear what she thought of his improper introduction of himself. He felt the urge to touch the fur again, but then controlled himself and drew his hand back.

"Such a beautiful woman, I could never hope... you look even better than in the pictures. So good of you to come! And at this hour too, aren't you afraid to be here, with me... in the dark?" He seemed never to blink his hollow eyes. The tone in which he spoke, the cadence of his voice - he might as well be a serial killer, she thought.

"I'm not afraid of men. I have what it takes to make them crawl at my feet," she said and looked him directly in the eye.

"Of course you do," he said. "I feel it, it emanates from your aura... Women like you are hard to come by."

She looked unimpressed. "Pardon my manners Goddess, I keep forgetting myself." He suddenly dropped to his knees and ran his long, lanky arms around her knees. She was caught by surprise with this abrupt display of submission, but she retained her composure, even when he pressed his face against the front of her leather skirt.
"What a Goddess you are! I have never met a queen as beautiful as you. All other women are just a waste of space... Only you... you understand my longing, you share my deep desires... If you make me do it, I will adore you forever."

His voice was muffled, as he was still pressed against the front of her legs. She could hear him breathing loudly, inhaling the smell of leather. He held her so tight, she was almost loosing balance. She looked around, as if she was trying to spot something in the surrounding woods that were pitch dark.

"Alright, where is your collar, slave? And your leash?"

"Oh, of course, Mistress." He at once let go of her legs and hurried to the closest bench where he had left his belongings. The name of the bag manufacturer, printed on a white reflexive rectangle, was the only thing visible in the dark. He returned in the blink of an eye with his collar in place, carrying his bag with him.

"If you care, my goddess, I will show you a surprise I prepared for you." She hesitated. Given his disturbingly awkward ways, he might produce a severed head out of his bag.

She eyed it suspiciously. "Um... right. But first take off your clothes. You are supposed to be naked anyway. I hope you are used to the cold."

He unzipped his trousers and in the flickering light of the old park lamp, the only one still working, he looked very pale. For some reason, seeing him naked made her think of the weird, ancient salamanders she recently saw in the ZOO. He lacked muscle mass and his belly was awkwardly protruding. His cock sprang up and even in the dim light she could tell he recently had been subjected to a Prince Albert piercing.

"For your sake, my Goddess."

"For mine and mine only?" she asked, a feeble, half-hearted attempt at flirting.

"Yes, there is no other woman in the world for me, just you. As I said, all other women are just flesh to me. Only you can own me as your obedient slave in mind and body for real."

"Alright, slave. Let's find them. Are you sure they're here? Even in this weather?"

"Positive, Mistress." The gray-fur lady attached the leash he was handing her and headed deeper into the forest, him walking few steps behind her.

"If we follow this path, we will reach their favorite spot." He spoke and his voice was constricted, trilling anticipation mixed with fear.

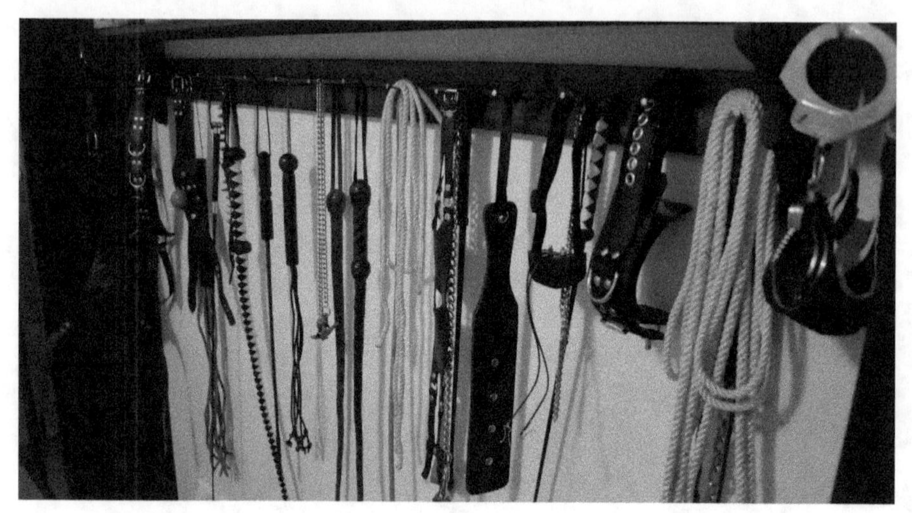

CHAPTER 6

2016

Tom had to dive into several layers of thin, rustling paper to realize, what was inside the cardboard box. A few seconds later he was staring into it at a pair of shiny stiletto shoes embellished with crystals, nested snuggly in fine black paper. They had a translucent platform and metal heel. Very provocative shoes, he thought, suitable for a pole dancer in a club or a high end sex worker.

Tom briefly checked his surroundings. No one was around and he took them out of the box. He realized the things were too large for a woman. There was a strap around ankle with a tiny lock on each shoe.

What he was about to do was insane, but he couldn't help it. He again looked around - the coast was clear, everyone was out for a lunch. He took off his smart low shoes and rolled down his socks. For a few moments he struggled to put the shiny things on, which was difficult without nylon stockings, but finally he slid in. He held the trouser legs high and checked himself in the reflection of the glass paneling of his office cubicle. The edgy shape of his legs and the dark hair above the veins around his ankles, all was in bizarre contrast to the shiny feminine sexiness of the shoes. It made for a pretty awkward picture. He realized that he looked like a pervert and hastily took them off and dropped them into the box as if they were cursed. When he was about to shut the lid on the box he noticed a red envelope, which slipped between the wall of the box and the layers of wrapping.

He examined it, handling it as if it was something either fragile or potentially deadly. It was a red envelope with the symbol of a shoe, Rebecca's unmistakable signature. He was opening it slowly, both aroused and terrified at the same time.

Hello Fuckboy,

I'm leaving for Dresden on business. I require my maid Priscilla to come to join me here. I have something special for her. Be sure to bring all her maid clothes, the new lingerie and these pretty shoes. I will meet you in front of the Marriott Hotel at 10 PM tomorrow morning.

PS: I hope you like your new shoes! Take them with you.

Your Mistress

Tom's arm slowly dropped to his side, the letter dangling helplessly in his right hand. She did it, she did it again... He fell back in his leather chair and glided down on the smooth surface.

The chair obediently inclined backwards to accommodate his movement. Rebecca was always keeping him on his toes with her little games, riddles and tasks. She knew his peace-loving nature and was always scheming to drive him out of his comfort zone.

Somehow, even though at the moment he didn't think so, when he looked over his shoulder he was very grateful to his Mistress, because he would never throw himself in the path of exciting things if it wasn't for her. The idea of traveling to another city for the "special occasion" seemed worrying nevertheless. What was it this time? He could expect just about anything from Rebecca when the whole Dominant Wives' Club was behind her!

CHAPTER 7

2016

Emma wore her hand-made business suit which accentuated her perfect hour-glass shape. She occasionally sported the Marlene Dietrich style and it was both smart and sexy. Her slave, his slave collar hidden under the turtle neck of his dark blue sweater, was trotting few steps behind her, carrying in each hand several designer paper bags. She walked side by side with Mistress Hannah who also looked great in her elegant dress, matched with short leather jacket. For a Lady in her mid-forties she had an exquisite figure.

That day, however, it was neither Emma's womanly shape nor Hannah's glorious tight ass that was the center of all attention.

The focus of everyone who they passed on their way to their favorite restaurant, was completely on the person carrying Hannah's shopping bags. People were staring, some of them openly, some covertly, many stopping in their tracks to gape.

"Move your lazy ass, Charlotte!" Hannah called over her shoulder, not bothering to look back.

"I have to admit, I wouldn't have the guts to walk around like that..." Emma, the seasoned Domina, almost blushed. "I guess you are far more the exhibitionist then I am. Or perhaps it makes me uncomfortable to irritate the less open-minded people..."

Hannah just laughed. "You are way too considerate of others. Look how they stare. This is probably the most interesting thing that happened to them in weeks. They will have something to talk about. And you know what?" Hannah grabbed Emma's arm and leaned closer for added emphasis. "They don't deserve your consideration... they wouldn't give you any themselves... You know my motto: Carpe Diem!"

Emma smiled and shrugged slightly. "I know you are probably right, but aren't you worried some hateful people might threaten you or resort to violence?" Hannah waved her hand. "We've never had any problems, not once."

Emma looked back at Hannah's slave, who was walking the shopping mall in a maid's uniform, complete with wig, stockings and heavy makeup. Charlotte looked very satisfied, enjoying the flabbergasted looks of the passers-by and swaying her hips to make her skirt move like a bell from side to side.

Emma couldn't help but laugh. "You two are incredible. My slave, Cunt, feels best when his slave collar is hidden under the turtle neck. I cannot blame him, I myself feel better when we look tolerably normal. Being as extraordinary as we are under the surface, I don't mind when we look normal on the outside."

"Well, I wouldn't venture out like this in Berlin, but in a different city I feel quite comfortable walking about with my Charlotte to do some shopping." Hannah stopped in front of the window of the restaurant on the upper floor of the shopping mall. "You two will do the groceries for the evening, we want to talk, just us girls." Mistress Hannah commanded. She handed Charlotte the shopping list and instructions for the dinner preparations and her maid curtsied.

Emma noticed that her slave Cunt didn't look particularly enthusiastic about walking around with a guy in a full sissy costume. Emma knew him so well, she could almost read his mind. He, just like herself, preferred to enjoy kink in private. Walking around and shocking vanilla people was against the grain for him. Emma looked him in the eye, sending his way the telepathic message: "Your friends enjoy this so much. You won't spoil it now, will you? You are not walking around dressed as a sissy yourself, so don't be a jerk."

Slave Cunt lowered his head, correctly interpreting her commanding look. Both Cunt and the sissy then bowed and walked away side by side, tall Charlotte towering on her high heels and swaying her hips on the crooked, but shaved manly legs.

Emma and Hannah walked into the restaurant. It was a nice, ambient place, decorated to conjure up the Mediterranean atmosphere. Low hanging designer lamps, dark furniture and unobtrusive music with Greek tones made one feel like spending an evening on the seaside, looking over the darkening water surface and not having a worry in the world. Both women took seats in the far corner of the restaurant for privacy. A handsome waiter served them crusty white bread with virgin olive oil, balsamic vinegar and an assortment of salty sticks, flirting unashamedly.

Emma checked her watch. "Rebecca will arrive any moment. I have some news, but I guess we should discuss it together." With a charming smile she waved away the waiter, who was looking for excuses to stay in their proximity and kept asking about their needs and wishes. "Those Greeks... Anyway, how is it going now with your slave? Are you still so busy at work or do you have more time to have fun just the two of you?" Emma inquired politely.

"Well, as you can guess, with two youngsters in the house it is almost impossible to enjoy good old kink... You can imagine now that you have kids too. You hate to give them bad examples. It would perhaps be beneficial for a girl to have parents in an openly Femdom relationship, but imagine how a boy's confidence might suffer."

Emma nodded. "I was also thinking about this. Bringing up girls in the spirit of Femdom perhaps might do them good, but would you like your own son addicted to Femdom and risk that he might one day fall prey to some of those less principled ladies among us? You know better than I do how many of those walk the earth."

Hannah tore a piece of bread and liberally dipped it in the olive oil. "I'm sure it is a pretty hot fantasy for guys to imagine mother and daughter Femdomming together, the younger learning from the older and establishing a family tradition of making the male family members into slaves,"

Emma laughed heartily. "That sounds like a pretty good plot for my next novel!" She smiled as the waiter served them rosé in beautifully polished glasses. "You are right, the older the children get, the more difficult it is to hide these things. Some time ago I spoke to a guy in his seventies, who recently convinced his wife to try Femdom. Their adult children somehow discovered the collection of BDSM toys and they were completely scandalized! These were adult children, mind you."

"Imagine how teenagers might react," Hannah snorted. "I guess all children like to pretend their parents have no sex life at all... now imagine they accidentally see their father crawling at the feet of their mom, licking the dirty soles of her feet... Well, who wouldn't be shocked?" They laughed again and at that moment Rebecca walked through the door.

Rebecca wore a black satin blouse and pencil skirt, a combination she knew was most flattering to her figure. Her high heeled shoes perfectly complimented her unusually small, gorgeous feet.

"You look stunning, Rebecca!" Hannah and Emma rose from their seats, exchanged aerial kisses. The waiter was in raptures now that the sexy ladies he was serving became three.

"I hardly remember your face, we haven't seen each other in ages." Emma pretended to scold Rebecca, who sheepishly cast down her eyes.

"I know! I traveled to Abu Dhabi for business and I had to deal with family issues."

Emma brushed her arm and shook her head to reassure her friend she was not mad with her. "That's life, and life is not always about Femdom," Hannah laughed.
"Well, it should be!" Rebecca ordered a Burgundy wine, because she didn't like Rosé. "Our Femdom regime took a back seat for a while. But now, I'm back in the game! I worked on the assignment you sent! I think Fuckboy is ready for this special occasion. My mindfuck methods are bringing results, I'm close to turning him into my perfect maid."

Hannah spread the napkin on her lap. "Well, we managed to keep everything under cover and they have no idea what we have in store for them! Are you going for truffle ravioli or clams?" She traced the menu with her finger. "Or do you like Mousakka?"

Rebecca hesitated. "Sounds suspicious. I hate seafood, isn't it an octopus meal?"

"It is lasagna, basically. A lot of delicious cream sauce and minced meat." Emma explained.

The Greek waiter took their order and when he was setting the cutlery on the table, Emma noticed a tiny necklace, plunging down into Rebecca's cleavage. "Is it what I think it is?"

Rebecca inconspicuously fished out the long silver line out from between her breasts. "Indeed it is."

"So is he now wearing a chastity cage around the clock?"

Rebecca laughed and tasted the wine, smacking her lips appreciatively. "Well, you know how it is... in the past he used to beg me to take away his orgasms and make him wear... you know..." She stealthily looked around, but no one was listening "... 'the cage'. But later he got second thoughts and implored me to free him again... I was too weak to insist. Or rather, I didn't see the sense in trying to break his resistance. Now he wears it, except for work. They have the damned metal detection door frames at work. But I recently devised a simple solution to forcing 24/7 chastity on him! I am so delighted he'll soon be in the cage at work also... thinking of my control over him."

The waiter served the truffle ravioli. "It smells divine." Emma beamed and the waiter smiled, showing his perfect pearl teeth that matched his snow white shirt.

"Only the best for you, special lady. I told the cook to give you extra truffles, because you brightened up my day."

Emma winked at Hannah. When he was leaving, she whispered: "Such a sweet boy, I'm tempted to get to know him better."

Hannah elegantly tasted her meal. "Hmmm... delicious... Do you realize he is probably just trying to get laid? That you are gonna be another in a long row?"

Emma smiled. "It is for the best to have clear expectations from the very beginning. Who wants lovers who get so desperately infatuated? That's one of the ground rules of being a hotwife, isn't it? You handpick lovers, who are perfectly in the know that you are happily married and nothing they do can change your mind. I saw men get so madly in love they would abandon their children and sell the roof above their heads for my sake. It annoys the hell out of me. The young studs are just out to have fun and so am I. It's a win-win situation."

Hannah smiled politely, but she wasn't much into cuckolding. She directed the dialog back to chastity, which was a familiar subject. "I remember, back in the day before we started to use chastity. My slave was trying to invent all sorts of feeble excuses. Mostly he complained that the ring was too tight or hurting his skin, or that the morning wood made him uncomfortable. But it just takes a bit of determination and proper management and he becomes as tame as a lamb, tending to my happiness, wearing his device for months on end... Of course he takes it off, when I want to use him for fucking..."

Rebecca gasped. Hannah pronounced the F word so loud some of the other guests in the restaurant looked up. The trio of friends giggled and clinked glasses, toasting to their bright Femdom tomorrows.

"I found out it is all about mind conditioning." Rebecca continued. "I also take it off sometimes for our evening sessions, so that I can tease him, but no -" she leaned lower over the table conspiratorially and whispered. "- no orgasms. I find he is incredibly obedient when the chastity regimen is in place. The key to reaping the benefits is in being pretty strict about it. We have a schedule and rewards system which keeps him motivated. He is willing to do just about anything when I promise him his reward. And I turn a deaf ear to his pleading." Emma patted her back. "That's my girl! You are making me proud!"

Rebecca beamed. "He told me once, when we were drinking at a bar, that he actually admires me even more when I'm strict and cruel with him. It took me some time to process that, but ever since he shared this with me, I take great pains to be as strict and demanding as possible. Of course I rather struggle with being cruel, but I'm getting there with enjoying that selfish control too."

Emma was munching on her delicious meal and washed it down with her rosé. "Hmmm, I know you somewhat struggle with the concept. But take me and Hannah as another example. We are having great success using corporal punishments, and pretty intense too."

Hannah nodded. "We are incredibly tuned to each other, Emma and I. That's why we often do BDSM games together. We are both pretty sadistic and our slaves have very similar level of pain tolerance. Being cruel and having fun causing them pain is one of the best things there is, especially when we know they enjoy being afraid."

"Yeah, isn't it curious? Deep down they desire to be very scared and unsure of how their Mistress will hurt them. It keeps them in awe of their Mistresses' dominance over them and reminds them of they are our toys."

Rebecca agreed. "I introduced cock beatings as punishment for late arrivals and also as preventative behavior maintenance... and it yields results! So, when are we going to tell them about tomorrow?"

Hannah shook her head, but her mouth was full, so Emma took over. "Well, we thought it actually might be a complete surprise."

CHAPTER 8

2016

Emma, Rebecca and Hannah were mounting steep stairs in a tall building.

"Oh," Hannah grunted, "why they didn't include an elevator in a building as tall as this I cannot comprehend!"

After reaching the third floor she was already panting.

"Wait for the view, it is so worth it!" Emma replied serenely.
"It better be, or next time your slave will have to carry my royal backside up the stairs," Hannah said playfully. Emma laughed and the echo of her happy voice rolled down the stairs.

"You are positively elated, Emma, why is that?" Rebecca asked as she stopped, breathing hard too. Emma slowed down to let her out-of-condition friends catch their breath. The corridor window was already promising a splendid view. The house towered over the Elbe river and the dusk colored the horizon in all shades of red.

"Well, today is Tom's maid initiation evening, how could I not be? I can't wait to see him in the whorish service uniform with all the bells and whistles," Emma chirped and impishly drummed with her fingers on the window railing. Rebecca smiled at her friend's sweet disposition, but something told her that was not all she had planned.

"Let's turn our volume down a little bit," Hannah hissed as other guests of the hotel climbed up the stairs. The mousy gray couple stopped speaking and pricked their ears, suspiciously eying the extravagant ladies as they were passing them on the stairs. They probably caught the part where Emma said 'whorish'.

Rebecca cupped her palm and whispered to Emma, "I know you, that's not the only thing that gives you such a mischievous look."

A Machiavellian smile played on Emma's lips and it was enough to raise goosebumps in any male who knew her.
" Well, I was just thinking about our boys and their blissful ignorance about what we have in store for them tomorrow evening."

Eventually, they surmounted the last flight of stairs and stood up against the only door of the top apartment. "I always book this particular condo, because it is the most private," Emma explained.

Rebecca pressed her forefinger against her full lips and Emma covered her mouth. Hannah laid her ear against the door and listened for a few seconds. "They are ready, the music is playing and I hear no steps."

Hannah gently and slowly pushed the door handle and opened the door. They were waiting for them. Entering from the brightly lit corridor, their eyes had to adjust to the dim light. There was no hall, they entered right into high, open space living area with a large window covering the whole wall.

Slave Cunt, maid Charlotte and maid Priscilla were standing in a row next to the door, awaiting their owners. When the Ladies entered, the maids curtsied. The slave dropped to his knees to welcome the Ladies with a respectful kiss on each shoe tip.

"Allow me, Ladies..." The maid Charlotte helped them out of their coats. Maid Priscilla was wearing a very pretty satin uniform and a curly dark brown wig that suited her complexion. Slave Cunt, unlike the other two, was wearing his customary slave uniform (nothing except his chastity device and a collar). Upon seeing the Goddesses, maid Priscilla froze like a statue, holding a tray with champagne glasses. She completely forgot why she was standing there in the first place, both terrified and thrilled by the prospect of realizing her long hidden and suppressed fantasy. How often he dreamed of wearing the complete sissy costume, sexy lingerie, a chastity device and heavy makeup in front of the superior Ladies! Sometimes when he masturbated, he envisioned that moment, but when he climaxed, he became so embarrassed about his fantasies. Now he was she... facing the reality of this mortifying vision coming to life! As the Mistresses entered the room, now she felt overwhelmed to really be the serving maid and felt like game blinded by the lights of a very real moment. She was paralyzed and an awkward pause ensued when she was supposed to hand the Ladies their champagne glasses.

Charlotte gave Priscilla an encouraging look and nudged her in the ribs. With a respectful curtsy, she bowed her head and then in a tremulous, high-pitched voice Priscilla finally said "M-m-may I offer you a drink, Mistress?" and clumsily pushed the tray with champagne forward. She silently cursed her jittery nature. The voice she was practicing tirelessly in front of the mirror, now sounded shrill and unnatural.

Rebecca took her glass and playfully pinched the rubber nipples protruding under the uniform of her humiliated, feminized husband. "I like your new boobs! They become you. Charlotte helped you with the make-up, didn't she?" Charlotte cast down her eyes modestly and battered her thick false eyelashes.

Rebecca turned to her own maid again. "How do you like your new shoes, little bitch?" Priscilla was doing her best to keep her balance on her sky high stilettos as she curtsied to answer the question, but the result was rather pitiable. "Uh... very well, Mistress Rebecca, thank you."

"You owe me something, don't you?" Priscilla set the tray with now empty glasses on a small table and dropped to her knees to hand to her Mistress the tiny keys to the locks on her fancy shoes. Rebecca took them and placed them carefully into a small pocket on her shirt.

Priscilla had no idea how difficult it would be to scramble to her feet again, wearing the super high shoes. She felt as silly, helpless and clumsy as a new born giraffe. She reminded herself that she was surrounded by predators as well and her survival depended on her skill to become a satisfactory sissy maid in shortest possible time. If she failed to meet expectations, her ass would learn a painful lesson soon enough.

When the welcome was over, the maids disappeared into the kitchen and slave Cunt accompanied them, to wait with them.

Emma lead the way into a spacious apartment with the other two Ladies right behind her. The character of the place was defined by an industrial spiraling staircase with a black railing. Candles were liberally set around the place, with tea candles two on each step of the stairs and in a neat row under the window.

"Wow," Rebecca breathed. They could see the dominant tower of the beautifully lit Frauenkirche. The flickering light of the candles didn't disturb the marvelous panoramic view of the city and accentuated the magical atmosphere.

The Ladies made themselves comfortable on the broad, black leather couch and Emma looked around, taking in all the effort their husbands had invested into making the apartment a place for a perfect Femdom evening. Hannah pointed at slave Cunt, who was kneeling in submission with his hands folded behind his back, at the disposal of the Ladies.

"Slave, play us the best of Agnes Obel," commanded Hannah. Slave Cunt promptly connected the audio system to his phone. He fiddled with the phone and soon a song by Agnes Obel surrounded them, setting the mood with a gentle instrumental melody.

Emma silently put her two closed fists together and pointed to the floor near her feet. This signal was called "Balls", one of ten body positions that Emma had trained her slave cunt to immediately assume. She had insisted slave Cunt master the distinct responses to her silent hand signals so that she did not need to waste her Superior breath talking with a slave about his body position. This one was also a cruel punishment position for receiving kicks, but today slave Cunt understood that Emma wanted him to serve as furniture. He quietly moved to the spot and got down on all fours to serve as her ottoman so that Emma could rest her legs on his back.

As Emma listened to the soft, contemplative singing voice, she spoke, "Good choice, I like Obel... Anyway, the refreshments are getting much better for us Ladies these days. I remember that some time ago when our slaves had no clue what to serve and what the appetizers should look like."

"Yeah, well, they learned from the best, one of the Cruella's slaves is a chef after all. That's the advantage of the Club. The slaves can learn from each other to live up to our expectations." Rebecca popped in a smoked salmon on a slice of cucumber, topped with lemon dill cream cheese and munched on it with the expression of ultimate pleasure.

Emma crossed her arms on her chest and with her thumb pointed to Hannah. "Did you know, that my dear friend here is the most avid promoter of sissification? She regularly organizes cross-dressing parties. As far as I'm aware you never attended one with Tom, am I right?"

"Right!" Rebecca conceded.

"Well, once a month she holds the maid training class. And today you have her experienced guidance just for yourself! You are in good hands, she will help you to turn your maid into the servant you didn't even dream about."

"I have no doubt about it, maid Charlotte is incredibly convincing! Anyway, why doesn't slave Cunt have a maid identity too?" Rebecca asked, hoping she wasn't stepping over some invisible border.

"I knew you would ask eventually," Emma smiled. "I was thinking of an answer that would provide you with a bit more insight than a simple sentence that he doesn't like it. So here I go. Let's say, that we, Ladies of the Club, believe in exploring the inborn possibilities of our slaves. In other words, we only work with the tendencies the slaves naturally have. Slave Cunt, unlike your man and Hannah's, does not harbor any potential to get feminized. Isn't it so, Cunt?" she addressed her slave husband.

"None whatsoever Mistress," he replied in his small, submissive voice.

"You obviously realize that even though it is called forced feminization, there needs to be pretty much the same level of consensus as with any other practice."

Rebecca mused on this for a while. She was still very much in the mindset of what fiction and porn taught about Femdom. Before she joined the Club, her knowledge was sketchy and she often found herself confounded by the omnipresent Femdom fiction and, even worse, by Tom's fantasies on the subject.

"Isn't that notion a bit too much consideration toward the slaves? Shouldn't we rule them and make them do and do to them whatever we please?" Rebecca asked slowly. She knew there are no taboo questions and other members of the Club will always answer any inquisitive inquiry without frowning upon her ignorance.

Emma smiled, very kindly, without a trace of condescension. "I remember you being the one, whose benevolence to the fastidiousness of your husband was ruining your Femdom life." Rebecca looked pensively out of the window, where someone decided to celebrate some worthy occasion with fireworks.

"Of course I understand what you mean, Rebecca," Emma continued when Rebecca didn't comment. "I see you. Now that you realized what Femdom is truly about, you don't want to repeat your old mistakes."

Hannah walked to the window and watched the fireworks

explode bright flickering flowers in the sky. She downed another glass of champagne. "In real life it all gets much more nuanced... It is not easy to navigate a Femdom relationship. It takes incredible determination, coordination and invention."

Emma joined Hannah by the window and the white fountain shaped explosions turned red and faded into glittering dust. The red illuminated their faces. "I quite agree," Emma said. "The absolute majority of us live with our slaves, they are our husbands and fathers to our children. There is only a handful of childless business women or professional Dominatrices, who keep a 24/7 slaves as domestic servants, but they are an absolute minority. We, dominant wives, need our slave husbands to be able to function in daily life. Not just function, but thrive. Our slave training is turning them into perfect slaves and husbands, but we want not, must not, break them and weaken their mind. I would approximate it to using black magic. The black magic is using the Female power to the extreme, to cause irreversible harm. We must never do that! We of course use mindfuck to make them obey and be submissive to us, but we do not break them. Their fantasies and kinky dreams are our tools we can use to make them compliant to our wishes... we seduce them into wanting to obey us because they find solace in the submission that we are in fact guiding. We believe in the superior skill of women to be the head of the family and the natural subordination of men. Women are wiser, more emotionally intelligent, resourceful and authoritative. But you cannot live in a relationship with a person whose mind is broken. It is not difficult to induce a lasting trauma and you certainly do not want to do that to your partner. Do you want to live with a spineless worm? Of course you don't. No one wants such a situation. That's where many subs get it wrong. By leading your submissive to the edge of their kink, they ache for it and will do anything of their seemingly 'free will' for us in order to experience their own fetish... that is how we Women dominate our male slaves. We make them obsessed to please us without question, in order for them to experience their own natural inferiority. As we Ladies savor the obedience and devotion we have cultivated in them, we dangle their fetish in front of them as a reward... and the circle of submission to our female dominance continues perpetually in their minds. They come to rely on being obedient to us, instead of lapsing into being selfish."

Hannah yawned and extended her arm around Emma's shoulders. "Emma, you are the ultimate philosopher of the Club, no one can possibly take that away from you, but please, let's just get on with it and see a nice maid exhibition!"

"Oh, but I do appreciate that Emma is always willing to clarify for me things about Femdom. I like the analogy to magic. Emma is the white witch, the agent of good! I sensed it ever since I met you, Emma."

Emma beamed at Rebecca's sweet, adoring eulogy, but Hannah snorted sarcastically. "Don't be so naive, Rebecca. You must not let her charm confound you. Emma has the looks of the sweet blond angel, but when she shares with you more of the stories of her wild youth, your eyes will pop out. Emma used to be the most evil of witches. It took her quite a while to become the agent of good." Hannah used fingers to draw apostrophes in the air at the phrase 'agent of good'.

"Hannah, Rebecca thinks I'm an angel and I quite like it, stop ruining it for her," Emma exclaimed in mock annoyed voice. "Alright, let's stop the nonsense, I want to see maid Priscilla boiling in her own juices, blushing in humiliation. Come on, don't say you are not looking forward to it too!"

Hannah took hold of and energetically twirled her riding crop. "Okay, but sometime you need to tell me how you turned from the evil witch to the good one!" Rebecca said to Emma.

"I most surely will, it is hell of a story. From the agent of good to the depths of hell and back again."

Hannah clapped her hands. "So, Rebecca, will you introduce to us your new servant?" Emma and Rebecca exchanged looks. Rebecca always looked to Emma for guidance and she gave her a conspiratorial little wink. They took hold of their riding crops as well. "Priscilla, down on your knees, NOW! Charlotte, I'm coming for you!" Rebecca called. From the kitchen sounded a shy, high-pitched "Yes Ma'am".

When Rebecca entered the kitchen, maid Charlotte made a polite little curtsy and continued slicing ham. She was immersed in her sissy role and clearly felt comfortable about it. Rebecca watched, spellbound, how her perfectly manicured hands were folding the cuts of ham and delicately setting them on top of sesame pastry. There was something utterly refined and gentle about her fingers. Rebecca stood next to her and stole one of the finished pastries, stuffing it into her mouth and munching on it happily. "Hmmm... so good! I doubt anyone can measure up as to the refreshments."

Maid Charlotte made a polite curtsy. "Always overjoyed to make the Ladies happy, Mistress."

"Bring the serving tray and come with me now into the other room."

The maid Priscilla was kneeling next to the dustbin with her head up and eyes cast down, patiently waiting for her Mistress to take notice of her, listening and observing. Rebecca finally turned to her own maid, intently looking into her face. "Great job, Charlotte! You helped my sissy to apply the make-up, right?" Rebecca praised her and Charlotte curtsied again, beaming. "Yes Mistress."

"I thought as much, my maid would never manage to do it herself!" It couldn't be seen over the heavy layer of make-up, but heat was raising up to Priscilla's cheeks. Rebecca skillfully fed Tom's natural competitiveness, kindling in him the desire to be better than the other maid. It was working. Tom almost got jealous at the high level of appreciation his Mistress was showing to the other guy, even though at that moment he was getting jealous of how Charlotte had helped feminize her as a new maid. Priscilla made up her mind that she would become just as good, or an even better sissy. Rebecca fastened a pink collar around her neck and smiled to herself how her little trick of flaming the fetish of her slave had worked, much as Emma had earlier described.

Kneeling Priscilla could feel the ankle straps fastened and secured with locks on her feet. As Mistress drew nearer, her kneeling maid's head reached only to her belly button. "Look at yourself, my personal maid, so ridiculous in your ladies' lingerie! Perfect little slut! Before the night is over, you will be fucked up your ass and all the other Ladies will watch you, laughing at you!" Priscilla's cock was tightly jammed in the chastity cage and when her Mistress talked to her like that, it was getting even more tight and painfully restrictive.

"Stand up and show my friends your maid attire." Priscilla rose to her feet and as she did was reminded of platform stilettos she was wearing that now increased her discomfort. Upon standing Priscilla curtsied. Her humiliation increased, as she stood up straight and was fully exposed to the Ladies who were smirking at the sight before them. Her body was coming alive and tingling with all the feminine touches that were a defining her presence now. Her nails had been painted a pink and they matched her lipstick. Strangely she could feel the thick glossy polish on her nails and taste the creaminess of her lipstick. Through her eyes, the view of the sexy Mistresses about to abuse her dignity, was framed by her false eyelashes. She remembered the deep eye shadow that maid Charlotte had applied along with full face makeup, and felt even more inferior and subservient standing before such powerful Women.

"Show us what you are wearing, maid," commanded Rebecca. Priscilla lifted her pink satin maids dress slightly to reveal a thick layer of black chiffon petticoat, with pink edges, that helped to lift the hem of her short skirt even higher over her thighs. She blushed, knowing that the Ladies could now see her pink garters with black bows holding the tops of her nylon stockings.

"Since you are such an exhibitionist, raise your petticoat higher for us also," Rebecca chuckled commandingly. When Priscilla did so, the Ladies could see her panties that were ornamented with layers of pink lace ruffles. They were crotchless panties and sticking right there out in front was her pink chastity cage framed by the delightful ruffles.

Mistress Rebecca pointed to her ankle, where a key was dangling on a delicate chain. Rebecca spoke haughtily, "What do you say sissy maid"?

Priscilla curtsied, "Thank you Mistress Rebecca for keeping my manhood locked away so that I focus on your needs and am not distracted by temptations to pleasure myself".

The Mistresses could not contain themselves any longer and burst out into laughter at this admission and the sight of the helpless new maid being indoctrinated into her sissy maid role.

Rebecca tugged on the leash. The maid scrambled and tripped forward, trying to keep upright. She was towering so high on her large shoes! Her step was wobbly and insecure as if she was walking on stilts. She was dragged into the middle of the spacious living area. "Ladies, allow me to introduce to you my new maid, Priscilla."

Long gone were the days when Rebecca blushed at the embarrassment of her husband in front of other women. She had learned to enjoy his predicament and laughed heartily at his feelings of shame and mortification. She knew already how deeply satisfying it was for him to contemplate and reflect upon these experiences later on, even if at the time he was experiencing it, he felt deeply uncomfortable. With each passing humiliation, he was becoming a much better servant to her, anxious to fulfill her every need. He hurried to repay her for the pains she took in turning him into the perfect submissive husband.

Priscilla, whose cock was desperately trying to get erect, felt like an electric impulse coursed through her. The agony of the high shoes, the tightness of the chastity cage, wig and make up, the restrictive clothes, corset hugging her middle section, all was sending the signal into her brain that she was the ultimate bitch and whore.

"Make a nice curtsy, Priscilla!" Rebecca commanded in a sharp, authoritative voice. Priscilla curtsied. "You will bow to the Ladies and show them proper respect!" Rebecca commanded and Priscilla dropped to her knees, bowing reverently. "Today you will get initiated into the ways of a proper sissy maid. The Ladies here agreed to provide me with instruction and guidance."

"Yes, we are quite pleased to," Emma smiled. "I will explain to your sissy Priscilla what is expected of her." Emma grabbed the ring on Priscilla's collar and navigated her to the open space.

Rebecca made an inviting gesture and to signal her ease, she comfortably leaned on the arm of an armchair, toasting with her glass. "I'm confident in your superior instructive skills, Ladies, you are free to do whatever you please with my maid." Rebecca winked at Priscilla and her cock twitched again.

Hannah pointed at Priscilla, who didn't know what to do with her hands. "You will pose for us. Think of a sex worker in a shop window."

Priscilla stood awkwardly in the middle of the room, but her eyes wandered to the corner, where oiled canes were prepared for use whenever the Ladies got displeased. She made up her mind. Better off embarrassing herself than having to feel Hannah's merciless hand administering one of her cruel punishments... She started to sway her hips and dance. Soon the Ladies burst out laughing. Dancing by Priscilla was an utterly ridiculous occurrence.

Emma refocused on her own slave, using him as a stool and twisting his nipples, listening to Hannah's instruction. "Your Priscilla needs to realize first, what it entails to be a sissy maid."

Mistress Hannah, her hips swaying, walked and stopped right in front of Priscilla, who, in the sky high shoes, was towering way above her. "Kneel down, now."

Priscilla dived down and supporting herself by her hands, she carefully knelt, trying to avoid toppling over in the high shoes.

"Much better," Mistress Hannah purred sweetly and delved her fingers deep into the locks of her wig. She stood so near Priscilla she could smell her leather dress.

"Sissy is a servant. Sissy is subservient. Sissy is a fucking doll. Repeat."

Priscilla tried to breath into her abdomen, but the tightly laced corset didn't allow her. "Sissy is a servant. Sissy is subservient.

Sissy is a fucking doll."

"The last role is probably the most important. I know you want it, I know you yearn to fulfill your role as a fucking hole on two legs. You desire to become the ultimate whore. Say it!"

Priscilla sighed breathlessly. She pressed her lips together. Hannah's smell, her perfume mingling with the smell of leather was infatuating. "I... I desire to... become the ultimate whore."

Hannah wandered with the tip of her riding crop between her legs and among the layers of her tutu found the cage. She stroked it slowly, at times touching on the bare skin of her sissy clit. "Ask me to teach you to become the ultimate whore."

Priscilla tilted her head backwards, the teasing, the dirty talk made her insane with lust. "Please, Mistress... Please... Teach me to become the ultimate whore. Make me a bitch for men, ready to get fucked."
Hannah nodded in appreciation. "I'm impressed! You, my little bitch, are getting it even further than I originally intended. Now listen intently. Look me in the eye."

Priscilla slowly refocused her eyes, blurry from the excitement. She felt almost hesitant to look Mistress Hannah in the eye, it took as much effort as looking into the sun and created the same urge to immediately turn her gaze away. Hannah's eyes behind the square eye glasses were stern and hypnotizing. Priscilla used all her willpower to maintain the eye contact for the whole sentence. "First and foremost, a whore must be the ultimate professional in seduction. How would you do that?"

Priscilla's head was spinning. Her mind was getting full of the sensual visions evoked by Hannah's words. She dropped her head, Hannah's eyes were too much. "Uhh... be very sexy... Mistress?"

"Right! You need to move sexy, behave sexy, make sexy expressions. Look at me." She moved her chin up. "Your movements must be fluid, elegant, you need to relax. Offer a smile of desire. Emma, please play us the erotic lounge playlist."

Emma took hold of her phone and soon a sensual strip tease melody filled the air. Hannah began to sway in the rhythm. "Think of yourself as a professional prostitute." She began to trace her body with the palms of her hands, into her crotch, over her breasts. "You will not earn a dime if you are not attractive in your looks, gestures, the way you walk." She took Priscilla's hands and raised her up. "Dance with me!" Priscilla tried to imitate Hannah's movement. Emma turned red, trying to stifle laughing. She didn't want to ruin their sexy dance, but Priscilla was stiff like a board.

"Relax, loosen your pelvis, bitch," called Rebecca. She got up and stood right behind Priscilla, grabbing her hips and making her sway her hips to the sides. "See? That's it, relax even more!"

Hannah danced to the rhythm, coiling her body. Rebecca was guiding Priscilla until her dance began to resemble a woman's. "You want to seduce men to desire fucking you!"

Priscilla nodded. She was beginning to get it and soon, she was swaying her hips all by herself. "You will practice, little bitch, and your Mistress will train you in achieving these female movements.

"Yes, Priscilla," Rebecca said, "You will practice, I will take care of that. I won't let you cut corners, you will become the sexy bitch I want you to be! You will work on it each and every day until you learn how a proper maid should walk and move!" Rebecca said, imitating the tone of Hannah's voice.

Maid Priscilla was feeling now, how the sternness in her Mistress' voice was somehow helping to turn off the rational part of Tom's brain and plunging him deeper into the subspace. He was beginning to feel more natural in his costume and his identity was, step by step, overpowering Tom. Priscilla stopped distracting herself by glancing to the window. She focused only on the instruction, on the voice of both Mistresses. She was living the moment as the apprentice maid Priscilla and his male identity was being pushed into the background.

"Now you will show the Ladies how are you getting used to your pretty shoes." Rebecca tugged on the leash and Priscilla attempted to walk, but her step was still clumsy and insecure.

"Ooooh, that won't do." Hannah pulled up Priscilla's tutu. "May I?"

"Serve yourself," Rebecca replied politely.

"This - is - not - how - you - walk." With each pause a stinging stroke by a riding crop landed to her bare thighs below her tutu and ruffled panties. Priscilla wailed. "Nooo, no Mistress, this is not how maids walk."

"Don't worry dear, maid Charlotte will teach you." Maid Charlotte appeared with a tray, carrying the refreshments. She laid it on the coffee table with an elegant, professional bow and, dancing effortlessly on her high heels, adopted a place next to maid Priscilla. Standing shoulder to shoulder, Hannah instructed maid Charlotte to do a catwalk to and fro. Charlotte obeyed and walked there and back again with swaying hips, purposefully overdoing each motion for the sake of instruction.

"See, maid? Look how Charlotte walks and try to imitate her!" Priscilla tried to replicate Charlotte's confident walk, but when she saw the reflection in the window, it looked completely ridiculous. She still looked like a giant crow, squelching in mud. There was something uncanny, disturbingly anomalous about her, trying to look and walk feminine. Her shape, her posture, the cadence of her step, all screamed - a man!

Hannah sniggered and caught Rebecca's hand, making a mock saddened expression. "Sorry love, but Priscilla doesn't have natural feminine talents. But don't you fret, with a bit of practice she will walk as sexily as my maid." Charlotte, proudly taking in the compliment of her Mistress, smiled - a bit smug. "What is that smirk? I don't recall allowing you to smirk, bitch!" Mistress Hannah barked and slapped her maid across the face. Maid Charlotte fell to her knees and begged for forgiveness in a dramatic, tearful voice. Rebecca watched silently, how Hannah's stern treatment registered with her sissified husband. He was clearly enjoying each second of the rough treatment.

"You know what the ultimate skill of each sissy maid is?" Hannah asked.

Priscilla bowed her head. Of course she knew, she was waiting for this subject to come up with the bittersweet feeling of anticipation and horror. "Accepting a good banging and giving a deep throat blow job." Priscilla responded, drawing deep satisfaction from speaking it out loud and clear.
"Impressive. You've done your homework. You get straight A's, dear Priscilla!"

"Now, let's see if your obedience is in line with your kinky mind!" Rebecca cooed and turned around. Priscilla watched her Mistress look over her shoulder. "I have a surprise for you. I think you will be so pleased to meet each other!"

Priscilla immediately woke from the trance. Was it what she thought it was...? Did her Mistress imply there is a man behind that door? A kinkster who gets all worked up from the idea of fucking a sissy? Tom was often toying with the idea of getting fucked by a man on the command of his Mistress. But! This was probably one of the only true hard limits he so far insisted upon. "Mistress?" He peeped. His mind was storming. Will another of his hard limits get conquered by his ever adventurous Mistress? With wide-eyed horror he stared at the door of the bedroom where Rebecca just pointed. He heard a suspicious sound and the door slowly opened.

CHAPTER 9

2016

Each of the Ladies was feeling pleasantly relaxed and relished the afterglow of the kinky evening. All of them were resting on the couch, the alcohol they drank throughout the evening having pleasurably sedating effects on them all. Rebecca's blouse was gaping open down to the fourth button and her lace bra peeped out. Her always flawlessly smooth hair styling looked ruffled and her stern rectangle eye glasses were resting on the coffee table. She didn't bother to fix her hair at this time, feeling a bit wild with herself. Priscilla privately thought the laid back style became her. The servants pushed the couch to the window so that all the women could enjoy the marvelous view of the city. With the lights switched off, night was glowing bright and the darkness in the room drew out the splendid panorama of Dresden. The reflection on the surface of the river magically erased the marking line between up and down. The Ladies didn't insist on the maids doing the dishes at this time and they sat at their feet, enjoying the precious moments of idleness and ease, that are so far between in their Domme households.

"The reflection makes me think of parallel universes. Have you already heard about the theory of the multiverse?" With food service done, Hannah's slave had changed into his casual slave clothes - leggings with net top tank. Together with his clothes went the maid identity. Chilling at the base of Hannah's armchair, he switched to his everyday personality. Without the maid make up he looked suddenly very plain. Now just the residue of the red lipstick on his lips reminded everyone that a mere twenty minutes ago he was incredibly convincing sissy maid.

"Well, in each and every one of the parallel universes you are my slave for eternity. You better get used to that," Hannah quipped.

Her slave hasted to assure his Mistress that he would never wish for anything else. "I just thought that perhaps in one of the other universes I might actually be a house-bound slave... I would very much enjoy that."

Hannah made him shift his position to set her feet on his lap. "Well, in another universe I might have chosen my study subject more wisely, and instead of becoming an HR specialist, I might have ended up a top-tier lawyer with tons of money," Hannah mused.

Emma looked at her in surprise, because she wasn't used to Hannah resorting to self-criticism.

"Well, until we find out if I have a rich aunt who desires to make me the heiress of her spectacular riches, you will have to slave for me both at home AND at work," Hannah joked. Everyone laughed, except Priscilla.

Priscilla wasn't listening to the chit-chat. She still lingered in the afterglow of her maid initiation ceremony. Her mind was filled to the brim with the experiences of the evening. She was trying to remember every detail - the gratifying smell of Mistress Hannah's perfume, the sensual touch of Emma's spidery fingers on his thighs, the intoxicating taste of Rebecca's butthole. She still wore her complete maid costume. It just felt right to stay in it for some time more, but in his head he gradually started to refer to himself as 'Tom' instead of 'Priscilla'.

In the course of the evening he was on the brink of coming so many times he couldn't even count it. He recalled the intense feeling, when Mistress Emma approached him and tied a satin scarf around his head, blindfolding him. It was right after they opened the bedroom door and he suspected that there was someone waiting for him in there. His sense of touch and smell had grown stronger with the blindfold as he was perceiving the scene only through his remaining four senses. The Ladies surrounded him and pushed him slowly forward to the bedroom, giggling mischievously. He didn't know who or what was waiting for him inside... With Rebecca his wildest dreams were materializing out of thin air. It happened so many times already! He realized none of the things he confided in her were lost on her. Sooner or later she used the things she learned against him and both his dreaded and desired fantasies turned to reality.

"Hey... Priscilla! Are you listening?" Rebecca interrupted her train of thoughts.

"Sorry, Mistress?" Priscilla jabbered.

"I said, it seems that you are not listening!" Priscilla blushed and promised to take part in the conversation. Rebecca used the opportunity to change the subject, she was very curious about Emma's past and she still heard just a tiny portion of it so far. "Emma, I sometimes think about the things you told me at the Femdom weekend, you know, about the cottage party with Mistress Chiara and how you spent the night in the old textile factory. But you didn't tell me how it all turned out..." Rebecca said.

Emma's head was slightly dizzy from all the wine she'd been drinking. She pinched the bridge of her nose, but no memory came back.
"Ah, that... Remind me where did I end with the story last time? I fail to recall."

"Sure, you left the party, because Cruella found out that Chiara took money from the slaves, who attended. Remember?"

"Yeah, of course. The treacherous bitch was deceiving her friends to make money. I told you how she was using me in her place and making slaves pay for my dominance? It is making my blood boil even now. Such insolence..."

Hannah's slave, who half an hour ago was a sissy maid, spoke again in his male voice and most people would never believe that he could possibly be the same person. "How come these people don't realize that their low-handed behavior will backfire sooner or later? Upon my word, if I was there back then I would take care of her."

Mistress Hannah rolled her eyes. "Stop trying to making yourself attractive to Mistress Emma. You keep forgetting you are my slave, not hers."

Hannah, one of the most confident women that ever walked

the earth, wasn't jealous about her slave's affection for Emma. She wasn't ever jealous and her husband loved that about her. Emma's spell was such he couldn't help himself but court her at any and every opportunity. Hannah commented on his efforts with good-natured laughs. They all had common understanding that flirtation is completely harmless and even welcome in their D/s interactions.

"Thank you, brave knight," Emma winked at him.

"After the night in the textile factory Severin returned to his wife and I got back to Köln. I told you already that my mom tried to reach me. She found out I had missed out on school for many weeks! I knew that the fun was over and I'd have to fix the mess I got myself into."

Hannah, who never sugar-coated her sharp observations, proclaimed "I have a daughter of the same age now. I would break both her legs before she would act up like you did!"

Emma laughed sadly. "Well, you're nothing like my mom. My mother failed to control me. No wonder though, I'm extremely head-strong and unyielding to any form of pressure. I was so obstinate she couldn't possibly tame me, unless I myself wanted to."

"It must had been hard - facing the threats of getting kicked out of school..." Rebecca, who was empathetic, never failed to provide support and would always say the right thing at the right moment.

"Well, if it was just that, I would call myself lucky. But my friend Mathilda, who all the time posed as my bestie, actually did a number on me."

Rebecca stared. "What did she do?"

As soon as Emma returned to her story, Priscilla's mind drifted off again. Tom was interested in Emma's story, but the memory of the most delicious kinky evening was still invading his waking thoughts. How could he possibly resist remembering it in his mind? He was there again as Priscilla, he felt the rush of becoming she, defenseless, vulnerable, locked in her ridiculously high heels, in a tutu and false boobs with the chastity cage. She felt the electric impulse of sexual fever coursing through her crotch when Mistress Hannah had encircled the ring of Priscilla's cage with her slim fingers. The way she forcefully pulled the cage forward, while Emma propelled her forward on the thighs with a snap of her whip.

Priscilla could feel in the air, or perhaps could tell by listening to the clapping of the heels, that they had entered a much smaller room. Priscilla could smell something peculiar. For a moment she struggled to identify what it was, before realizing it is the smell of peach flavored lube. Was there just the four of them? Priscilla and the three Dommes, or was there someone else? Mistress Rebecca pulled her forward and soon his knees stopped against a high mattress. "Climb up, bitch!"

"Uh.. Yes Mistress." Priscilla fumbled blindly in front of her and was trying to make sense of the surrounding space. She climbed up.

"Now, on all fours! I want you to meet my friend Justin! Priscilla's blood froze. "Justin?" she peeped in high voice.
"Yes, Justin! Didn't you tell me - last week - that you secretly desire to get fucked up by a horny male on my command?"

"Uh... Yes Mistress I recall."

"Are you trying to tell me that you are such a sissy coward that you can't do it, now that my horny friend is here?"

Tom was trying to take over the mental reins and stop the inner turmoil that was raging under the surface of his submission. Rebecca sensed his apprehension.

"I command you to stick out your ass and get pounded by Justin. That's what you were trained for, remember? I order you to get laid by Justin, you will hold your ass open for him and take his cock. Do you understand?"

CHAPTER 10

2016

"Priscilla, we ran out of wine, go and get us some more," Rebecca commanded. "There is the last bottle of rosé in the fridge," whispered Hannah's slave, who was taking care of the wine serving when he was maid Charlotte.

"Yes Mistress." Priscilla, who was allowed to have some of the wine as well, tried to put into practice the sexy walking lesson she learned and the Ladies cheered at her attempts. She was getting better and better each time she tried.

"She is almost ready - be sure to practice some more during the day tomorrow. Don't forget about the essential commands, that we didn't cover yet," Emma whispered to Rebecca.

"Don't prick your ears Priscilla, move your ass now and get the wine," Rebecca called out sharply, because her maid slowed down - clearly trying to catch what they were conspiring about. Priscilla jerked herself back into action, embarrassed that she had been caught in the act and swiftly disappeared into the kitchen.

Priscilla used the opportunity of being out of sight to visit the bathroom. With the chastity cage it was impossible to pee in a standing position, so she had to sit down. As she sat down, she felt her sore anus and along with the ache came the thrilling memories of being fucked earlier that evening. The bubbly wine got into Priscilla's head rather quickly as she sat and closed her eyes remembering the events. Ahh yes... with her eyes blindfolded and on all fours, she was waiting for Justin to penetrate her. Priscilla began to feel her sissy cock twitch again, reliving the thrill and humiliation of the moment.

Suddenly it all came back... she felt someone larger climbing onto the bed behind her. She felt strong possessive hands on her butt grabbing to hold on to her hips. With her eyes covered, every touch was felt twice as intensely. Goosebumps raised up on her body, she felt her skin coming alive against the tight costume.

"Go ahead, Justin, you have my blessing!" Rebecca gave her approval for Justin to take Priscilla and there was an avalanche of laughter. Priscilla's head was pushed down and her cheek pressed sideways into the mattress. This caused her back to arch and raised her ruffled panty covered ass into the air in a position better exposed to receive his cock. There was no dignity now as the crotchless panties exposed her hole for all the Ladies to see. Priscilla felt how the well lubricated cock pushed against her anus, fighting it's way inside. Her anus was contracted, she still wasn't mentally in the place to allow him in.

"Relax your sissy cunt, bitch! Open yourself up to please your alpha male!" Rebecca commanded. Priscilla made the conscious effort to let the cock in and felt it glide inside, deeper and deeper. "That's better, fuck doll".

Finally the whole rigid cock was in and Justin began to fuck, first slowly, gliding in and out and stretching her anus. Priscilla, although used to getting fucked by Mistress, felt like her anus was in uncharted territory, a virgin hole, currently being claimed and stretched by the alpha's thicker cock. Her mind was blank, she felt like the ultimate fuck doll, unable to resist, expected to serve all the dominant alphas, male and female. Justin was working himself up, his fucking gaining strength and momentum, sending Priscilla into violent motion forward with each deep and forceful thrust.

Priscilla, still sitting with her legs spread on the toilet, realized that her cock is very hard, trying in vain to get erect in her cage. The humiliation she was experiencing at the time was shattering to the core, reaching the deepest layer of Tom's kinky soul.

"Priscilla?! Where the hell are you?" Rebecca's stern voice sounded from the living area. Priscilla hastily flushed the toilet. "I'm coming!"

"You better not be, bitch, or you will taste my whip! Just bring the wine!" Rebecca joked. Ladies laughed. Priscilla hurried to the bathroom to wash her hands. Proudly perched on the top of the washing machine was "Justin" the super realistic male doll the Ladies used to fool him. Rebecca was brilliant with mindfuck games... When the thrill of the moment was over and their little trick revealed to Tom's eyes, he was so very relieved. Rebecca knew him even better than he thought possible. Getting fucked by a man was one of the fantasies he found very arousing, but in reality did not wish to realize. Even though the illusion was thrilling at the moment, he would probably feel ill-used afterwards. Emma always said how incredibly dangerous that mind games might become if the hard limits get broken. He was proud, though, that Rebecca witnessed his resolution to obey her command. At that thought, he felt himself fall into a deeper level of submission to his considerate Mistress Rebecca.

Priscilla returned with the wine and her step in the shoes came across as elegant and certain. She served wine and even tried to mimic Charlotte's delicate hand gestures.

"Where were we? Ah, right - Mathilda. Long story short, she turned out not to be a very good friend," Emma said.
"You shared with her all your adventures? You told her everything about Adam, Chiara, what had happened at the cottage party and so on...?" Rebecca asked.

"Well, I had no reason to mistrust her, we were bosom friends for two years."

Hannah closed her eyes and her brows contracted. "You just had to get an unfortunate slap in the face from fate, right then and there. It surely spared you something much worse later in life..."

"Thanks, Hannah, I appreciate your wisdom," Emma sighed and Hannah smiled mildly, her eyes still closed. "You're very welcome."

Rebecca mused on what Emma just said. "After what you told me about her, it sort of makes sense. She had the money, but you had the looks. For women, looks are more than money. Always. She envied you being better looking than her. No money could buy her the attention and admiration you always got."

Emma nodded. "Good deduction. You are not far from the truth... So what do you think she did then?" Emma asked.
"I can only guess, but I have a feeling that she pulled the rug out from under you ..."

"Yeah. Don't ask me how, I have no idea - but she found the photo of me with the sissy maid at my feet, posing in Chiara's torture chamber. And what did - my best of friends - do with it?"

Rebecca slapped her mouth. "Oh no, she didn't..."

"Oh yes, that's precisely what she did." Emma rose and walked in front of the window. She felt that her energy was exhausted for the rest of the night, but it miraculously recharged with the renewal of her past agitation. She couldn't contain the memories just peacefully sitting there... "

"Mathilda pinned the photo on the cork board in our school. The next day everyone was talking about it. Shit hit the fan and... All the kids were pointing at me, laughing. I guess the worst for me was that they thought that being a Domina means to fuck each and every one of your slaves. I was a virgin still! This perspective was, and still is, incredibly offensive to me. Before the day was over, my parents knew."

Rebecca hid her face in her palms, horrified. "Oh no!"

"Hell yes. You can imagine my embarrassment. Luckily, at that moment I had Severin to lean on. I called him that very day. I must give him credit for what he did for me then – he hastened to my side and supported me throughout that whole purgatory experience."

Emma's slave was kneeling close to Emma, his hands resting on the calf of her leg. "I remember that, my Mistress. I picked you up from school with my car, as I had just arrived from Berlin. You were white as sheet and trembled all over. I remember how you grabbed my thigh in the car and dug your long fingernails - you wore them so long back then - into my skin. I knew you needed to let the steam out."

Rebecca leaned to Emma. "Awww.... I'm so sorry! And you had to face your parents too..."

"Paradoxically, facing my parents was easier for me than to stand up to the ridicule of my schoolmates. My parents were always way too kind. They couldn't measure up to my obstinacy and free will. All my life they tried hard to parent me with the authority I sorely needed, but it just failed to work. Long ago I established my sovereignty over them with my bossy ways and it was too late for them to try to take over the reins then."

Hannah shook her head. Her experience as a mother of a teenager made her perspective different and she could feel for Emma's parents.

"When my mother tried to make me ashamed for what I did, I reminded her that she herself left my father to live with a woman. She drove my father to commit suicide, remember? How can anyone, doing things like that, admonish me?" Hannah's slave was anxious to take the right side. "Indeed! How could she admonish you?"

Emma patted his cheek. "Good boy. I like you even if you don't constantly try to win my approval, darling." He blushed and stopped interrupting. "My parents made me feel so guilty of their parental failures that in the end, I ended up convincing them it was all their fault. I was completely fierce and unforgiving with them. They tried to make me penitent, but instead, I made them penitent."

Emma sensed how this stung Hannah, who was currently going through teenage parenting purgatory herself.

"Hannah, I feel for you. Of course I see it differently today. Being a parent shifts your perspective. I recently apologized to mom and dad for my utter lack of humility. I was too hard toward them. We have such high standards for our parents, how can they ever measure up? Leaving the parent/child equation out of it, one should never admonish others without walking in their shoes. I know that now, Hannah. You know, I do."

"Some years ago you talked differently, but we all have to grow up some day!" Hannah said. "Glad to hear you talking sense."

Emma knew that it was a sensitive subject, because Hannah was just in a middle of a parent/child crisis.

"Get back to the story Emma, Rebecca wants to hear the rest of it, look at her, it is written all over her face."

Rebecca quickly composed herself, curbing her all too obvious curiosity and Emma continued. "After my parents admitted, they were at fault for me being a brat, we still had to go to school and see if the institution would allow me to continue to the Abitur. Of course my parents had to take over the negotiations. I resolved not to intervene. The next day the three of us went to school. It was a break when we arrived and all the kids at the corridors pointed at me, I was mortified! We were led to the headmistress' office. I could hear the nasty hissing of girls and laughs of boys. It was for the first time in a quite a while, when I felt completely powerless. My parents talked about me with the headmistress as if I wasn't there, as if I was being admitted to a mental asylum. My father valiantly tried to make a case for me, solemnly swearing that henceforth I'm going to be as docile as a lamb. My mother brought up my superb study results... But then something unexpected happened. I was perfectly equipped to withstand harsh and stern treatment, but the Headmistress was actually being very kind! That totally took the wind out of my sails. The fat lady offered me a chance to mend my ways and was willing to let me do the Abitur if I attended school without failure in the remaining four months before the exam."

"Considering that you now have a doctoral degree, I assume that you just stuck it out, and graduated?" Rebecca asked as she smiled.
"Yeah, I bit the bullet. Honestly, the headmistress and her incredibly supportive and understanding approach did the trick. It was as if the fierce animal in me, the raging monster, was lulled to sleep within me."

Rebecca calmly nodded. "So ... the headmistress understood. I guess she took the pains to learn about your circumstances."

"Yeah, I guess she knew about the suicides and my lesbian mother and she saw me for what I was - an enraged teenager trying to survive the turbulent situation. She is long gone from this world, but I'm taking my hat off to her." Emma took off an invisible hat and made a bow, with her eyes to the ceiling. "She is the person I can thank for finishing my education. In the end I graduated with straight A's."

"Of course you did. And what happened to Mathilda?" Rebecca asked.

"That's a story for another day, but I made her shut her mouth once and for all. Not very proud of that to be honest, but at least she would never ever do any harm to me or my reputation. No, I'm serious, don't make me say anymore now. It is getting late and don't you want to enjoy this little drama over a cup of coffee?"

Hannah, resting her head on the backrest of the couch smiled,

her eyes still closed. "Yeah, true. Wait to see what your saint Emma can do."
Rebecca gave up and didn't insist anymore. "Alright then, but you piqued my curiosity! So at least tell me, what happened with Severin?"

"Hey, Cunt, tell Mistress Rebecca what happened then."

Slave Cunt blushed deeply and seemed hesitant.

"No, no, no. I will do it instead" Emma said, changing her mind. "You might try to make yourself look better and that wouldn't do."

Slave Cunt laid his forehead on the couch, clearly ashamed.

"Well, it was one week that we had spent together. He was staying at a hotel - he had to take a week off from work to come to Köln and he said to his wife that he was going on a business trip, so she wasn't calling him a thousand times a day as she did when she was suspicious that he was with me. Priscilla, pour me another glass - I returned to school and he would pick me up every day and we rambled around the Köln cemetery. He proclaimed his undying love to me, and promised he would become my slave forever and ever. I believed him! Didn't I, Cunt?" Slave Cunt dived down and began to kiss Emma's feet, he was red in the face and his ears turned pink.

"Each afternoon we shut ourselves at the hotel. We had the 'Don't disturb' sign hanging on the doorknob for hours on end. Slave Cunt smiled and looked over the heads of others, his gaze unfocused. "I remember the hotel. The doors were set so high on their hinges one could see feet walking the corridor around our room. Other guests probably could hear us too. I remember how we walked out of the room at one occasion and an elderly lady gave us beaming smile and whispered 'Be naughty while you can!'" Emma laughed fondly at the sweet memory.

"A kinky grandma! That's sweet! Perhaps she was a Domme in her heyday!" Hannah said and offered her other bare foot to her slave for a massage.

"Right behind the door, Severin used to drop to his knees. He was in his early thirties at the time, fit and athletic from the gym... I ordered him to take off his clothes. Wait - I have a photo somewhere... I have it saved in my favorites." Emma briskly swiped the screen of her phone. "There he is - look."

Rebecca leaned closer. It was slave Cunt, but much younger. He was gazing, starry-eyed, somewhere beyond the horizon, bare chested and wearing a thick slave collar with a tiny jingle bell attached to the D ring. Rebecca had to admit that he look very sweet, his boyish charm reminding her of Jamie Dornan. He didn't look remotely his age not then and not now.

"He treated me with so much reverence, I felt like a queen. The spark between us was so strong we couldn't get enough of each other. He was so skilled with his tongue he made me come over and over. He worshiped my body for hours, he loved licking my feet and rimming my anus, in short each and every form of homage one should pay to a Dominant Lady, he bestowed upon me. I adored it! You know what's curious? We are still so attuned to our respective roles, we never drop them. Some of the other couples don't stick to their roles in civil lives, but we do, and always did. Of course, that does not apply to Hannah here, she of course is a Domina with every fiber of her being, she never drops her role either..."

"And you still managed to go to school, I gather?" Rebecca wondered.

"Of course I was dutifully going to school and he was taking care of my errands in the meantime."

"Judging from your expression, your bliss didn't last long."

"No, you are right there. One day I came from school and he wasn't there to pick me up. Instead, a little schoolboy - I can still see his bright green jacket - gave me a letter from Severin. I don't recall what it said word to word, but it was something around these lines:"

Emma cleared her throat and started to narrate:

Dear beloved Princess Emma,

You know that my heart and soul belong to you. It is therefore incredibly painful for me to write you this letter.

I know it's cowardly not to tell you and look you in the eye when I tell you, but I'm not equal to it, I just can't.

Regardless of what I feel, I'm still married and my wife has not a single other person in the world, no one, aside from me. You have your parents who are not perfect, but they love you dearly. Ulrike, however, has no one to turn to. I must be there for her, she is mentally very fragile and I must protect her.

You are strong and can fend for yourself! I admire you for it so much. But from now on I will do my best to root out my submissive nature and numb my desire to serve you. I must become the man my wife needs. I will never ever see you again, and no other dominant woman for that matter.

I believe you will understand, you are one of the cleverest and most acute women I have ever met.

"Did I forget something, Cunt?" Emma looked at the slave at her feet.

"No, Mistress, you got it perfectly. Only in the end there was 'I'm going to love you forever'." He added in a small voice.

"Well yeah, right, that's very romantic," Emma retorted. It was clearly painful, even after all those years.

Rebecca looked sternly down on slave Cunt. "I see you. Such a disappointment burns right into your heart!" "I never was that hurt in my life, perhaps aside from the damn Ernesto," Emma agreed.

Hannah smirked a little. "Clearly you hadn't been through much in your life up to that point."

Emma slapped Hannah's thigh.

"What?! It's true!" Hannah exclaimed. "After all we'd been through, I was falling in love with Severin. And now? He just disappeared. Don't you recall how dramatically you experience the first heartbreaks? The damn letter... I must have read it thousand times. Needless to say I cried into my pillow for several nights."

Slave Cunt stroked Emma's calves, just as if it might attenuate his sin.

"At the tender age of eighteen that must had been very disheartening!" Rebecca patted Emma's arm, an empathetic gesture, accompanied with a sad smile.

Emma returned her smile with gentleness that she reserved for the most faithful of her friends. "Fortunately, I didn't have the time to pine for him for too long. I had Abitur ahead which I took seriously. Before I knew it, the high school was over and the Abitur successfully behind me. I tried to push the memory of Severin to the back of my brain. After all I was young and I had an amazing carefree summer in front of me! Two months of liberty before I went to the college in Berlin! Is there a better time of your life than that? You know how it feels... you think the world belongs to you. But the disappointment was still buried somewhere deep within and it drove a change in me that wasn't for the better."

"Well, most of us made use of this special time by partying hard, drinking, hanging out with friends, but not dear Emma, no, Emma instead set about to create her own cult." Hannah said somewhat sharply.

"Well, I just thought, the best way not to get exploited ever again was to get to the top of the pecking order. So, I left Köln far behind with my parents scratching behind their ears. For a few months I transformed into a dutiful daughter, but once the school doors closed behind me, there was no holding me back. Unlike Severin, who returned to the state of denial," Emma said as she gave him a significant glaring look, "I was resolved to taste and try all flavors of Femdom and explore everything there was to enjoy."

"That sounds a bit scary, knowing you," Rebecca quipped.

Emma gave Rebecca a sideways glance and impish smile played around her mouth. "Should I tell you what I did when I got to Berlin? It is quite a story..."

Hannah interrupted her, clapping her hands and began to raise from her place. "Ladies, I will employ my authority as the oldest Mistress and call it a day. We should get our beauty sleep! We can all talk about Emma's insane adventures tomorrow." Hannah strolled lazily to the kitchen. Emma leaned towards Rebecca and whispered loudly: "Hannah doesn't approve of the teenage me.

She thinks I was an insufferable brat."

"I can hear you, and yes, you were insufferable brat," Hannah called from the kitchen.

"Sorry, Ma'am, yes Ma'am," Emma called back jokingly in a sing song voice. "Hannah is for all purposes my adopted Femdom mom. She has a point - I was intolerably arrogant, entitled and..."

"... and devilishly sexy," said slave Cunt, who was anxious to obliterate all the traces of bitterness, revoked by the narration of his past shortcomings. Emma patted his cheek, but there was too much energy in the gesture so it felt rather like a face slap.

"Good try. I'm not the one you can win over by cheap flattery; you should already know that. Better that you go and prepare my bath before bed now."

Emma sent slave Cunt away and leaned to Rebecca. "I have something you may find interesting, Rebecca. From the large pile on my desktop I recently excavated my old diaries. I thought you might like to read them, so I brought one, covering my teenage years. I think it makes a rather interesting read."

Rebecca laid her right hand on her heart. "Oh, if you trust me with your own diaries, I am honored!"

"Of course I do... I think it makes for a nice read before bed. I will send slave Cunt to bring it to you. Now let's get some rest. Tomorrow's gonna be a very eventful day."

Rebecca looked Priscilla directly in the eye. "You are right, Emma, it's going to be very, very eventful day."

Priscilla didn't like the suspicious emphasis Rebecca put on 'very' and how she deemed necessary to repeat Emma's statement and mouth it so conspicuously as if she thought Priscilla was half-witted. Looking for reassurance, Priscilla sought the eyes of Mistress Emma, but she was all innocence. Perhaps she imagined it... but after all she'd been through, Priscilla thought her suspicions of more limits being pushed were all but unfounded.

CHAPTER 11

2007

Emma sat astride the back of a very hairy naked slave. She went full throttle in a dangerously sexy latex dress and brightly red lipstick. She changed position to cross her legs while she sipped Pina Colada. A fetish show was underway, where a tiny girl in green latex, aptly named the Wasp, performed trampling choreography on a large, bulky man, entertaining the whole party.

The Club was full of Femdoms of all shapes, wearing all sorts of fetish clothes. Emma, who arrived in Berlin a month ago for her summer vacation, was comfortable in the company of her new house slave and observed the buzzing around her. She paid no attention to the disparate trampling couple and her eyes feasted on the extraordinary and often bizarrely dressed women and their slaves. One particular person caught her eye.

"Matthew, who is that?" Currently serving as a living stool, the first house slave strained to turn his head in the direction his Mistress pointed. It was difficult in the current position and with the leather collar on, but he strained his neck further until he managed to see in the direction she pointed. Emma apparently thought her slave would recognize the elderly Lady with elaborately curled gray hair in a long velvet dress adorned with glittering crystals. "I have no idea, but the Lady seems to remember the flood of the world, Mistress," the slaves whispered.

"That's a pretty disrespectful thing to say," Emma frowned. "I thought perhaps you know her, being familiar with the Berlin fetish scene."

Coming to watch the show from a closer distance, a petite pretty Lady sat right next to Emma on a bar stool. Emma was so intrigued with the peculiar elderly Lady, she didn't notice that the woman who just joined her, was the very same Mistress who attended the infamous Femdom weekend, where Chiara exploited Emma for her material gain. Had Emma noticed her, she would probably have left. She didn't desire to engage in conversation with anyone who was the friend of Mistress Chiara.

Too late. Valeria noticed Emma and exclaimed in the way one does when meeting an old friend: "Oh, hey Emma! We met year ago at..." Emma cut her short.

"I recall."

Valeria looked slightly taken aback by Emma's cold tone. Emma, looking at her innocent, bewildered face, realized that Valeria perhaps doesn't even know what happened back then. Chiara certainly didn't brag about her being a mercenary bitch and explain the sudden departure of Emma and Cruella by some honest reason. Emma stopped frowning and decided to act at least cordially polite and made the effort to get the conversation flowing again.

"Who is the Lady over there?" Emma asked and pointed to the elderly Lady.

"No idea, but she seems to come from the time when the wheel was invented," said Mistress Valeria innocently.

Emma looked at her, scandalized. "I hope I will look like this when I'm in my seventies! Isn't it cool to imagine that being seventy we can still hang around doing kinky stuff?"

"Well, I don't want to rain on your parade, but the creature looks more like ninety..."
Emma was forced to concede that it could be the case. "Oh, dear, she even has a slave of her own!" Valeria said and sounded almost disgusted.

"See? There even is a slave who appreciates good old wisdom!" Emma said. The old Lady finally noticed that the two women were staring her way. Emma sent her an aerial kiss, and smiled to shun away the embarrassed feeling of whispering, pointing and gossiping about her. Emma dropped the subject immediately, but from time to time she shot a curious glance in the way of the peculiar Lady. She was training her slave, who wore a hood. He was chubby, but surely many, many decades younger than her.

Before the night was over, the Lady approached Emma. "Excuse me, do we know each other?" she said, "Were you laughing at me, or with me?"

"Oh, um, I mean... of course with you, not at you!" Emma stuttered, because right at that moment she realized that the Lady was not a lady at all. Her voice was way too deep for that. Emma tried to cover her perplexed reaction with a disarming smile. "I mean, I admired you perfect hairdo and how magnificently you look in that dress!"

"Oh, that's awfully sweet of you! I've been around for quite some time, but this is the first time someone flattered me like that. Now, sweet child o'mine, my name is Irina, but you can call me your fairy godmother. I will grant you any wish." Irina winked at her theatrically like old time movie star.

Emma shook hands with Irina and suddenly all the embarrassment was gone from her. "How old are you? Eighteen?"

"Nineteen, actually." Emma corrected and moved to sit between the shoulder blades of her huge-backed slave, so that Irina might sit on his lower back. Valeria gave Emma a skeptical look and ventured to obtain another cocktail.

"Charming... The generation that is sucking the kink right from the breast of their mothers..." Emma jerked herself.

"Excuse me?"

"Never mind, child. Good to have such a young beauty in our midst."

Emma knew better but to wave down the well-intended compliment, but it made her feel weird anyway, so she changed the subject.

"I take it you are pretty seasoned attendant of the Berlin parties, Irina?"

"Well, usually I throw parties myself, but it happens occasionally that I venture out to a party like this... You see, I run my own BDSM studio, the oldest in Berlin, I'm proud to say. If you ever happen to find yourself around the Tiergarten subway station, be sure to ring me, here's my business card. The whole of Berlin is coming to enjoy my vast collection of toys, gadgets and fetish clothes. I know most people here... My intuition, surely as developed as yours, tells me that you've been to Berlin only recently."

Emma raised her eyebrows slightly and then frowned a little. "Am I so conspicuously alien?"

"I was watching you. Your body language discloses that you are a cosmopolitan sort of girl, but you know only a handful of people here. Not to worry though, I will be happy to introduce you to some interesting people. I know an awful lot of gossip if you are into that."

Emma thanked her, thinking that she would probably not make use of Irina's offer - she made new friends effortlessly and needed no assistance.

"Now when I think of it, there is one thing you might help me with. Do you know Lady that goes by the name of Mistress Chiara?"

"Most people know her around here. Are you interested in her? I know things that will make you shudder." Irina was enjoying herself, glad to be the middle of Emma's attention.

"Indeed?" Emma's eyes widened, but she curbed her enthusiasm lest she discourage Irina from sharing more details with her.

"Yes. And your eyes will pop out when I tell you what I know."

CHAPTER 12

2016

There was a gentle rap on the door of Rebecca's and Tom's room. As Tom was currently in the bathroom, Rebecca opened the door. Her plunging neckline and her plump bosom made for a very attractive look - the satin was covering enough for her to look elegant, not vulgar, but sexy enough to make a male fantasy soar. Slave Cunt, who was holding a book on the palms of his open hands, made a focused effort not to stare at her decolletage.

"Sorry to disturb you, Mistress Rebecca, my Mistress is sending you this."

Rebecca thanked him, silently appreciating his self-control (she was used to males staring at her boobs).

Henceforth, Rebecca's attention was exclusively on the inconspicuously bound notebook, which promised to contain the fascinating read of Emma's life. Rebecca crawled into the bed sheets and with a self-indulgent purring delved into the pages. After the busy and exciting day it felt soothing to relax her limbs. The bedding was soft and smelled fresh. A glass of wine was already waiting on the bedside table. She could hear Priscilla, who had transformed back into her husband Tom, taking the shower. Rebecca had the time to immerse herself into Emma's story before the evening slave service.

Ever since Rebecca learned about Emma's eventful life, she was insatiably curious about her journey as a dominant woman. She devoured every particular detail of her life and felt gratified each time she learned something new. She barely knew why - generally she paid no interest to gossip. She didn't follow tabloids, didn't give a damn about Kardashians or whoever was now in the spotlight. Yet she idolized Emma. Was it her special something, or was she in some weird way in love with her? Was it just curiosity in bizarre stuff, to attempt look under the lid of other people's kinky lives? Neither, she decided. She simply tried to emulate Emma's ways and absorb some of the coolness factor that emanated from her. Emma was in all situations so self-assured, yet kind and without a trace of condescension. She effortlessly navigated the D/s scenes, yet she had a very warm and affectionate relationship with her husband. Analyzing her friend and her experiences, she hoped to become such an amazing Domme herself - stern, methodical and passionate, yet kind and tolerant when the situation warranted.

Rebecca could hear Tom brushing his teeth and humming a gentle melody. She smiled and thought the day had turned out perfectly - all she planned worked out magnificently and there was another surprise for Priscilla still to come. Rebecca derived great pleasure from taking Tom's breath away. She sipped a mouthful of the wine and held it in her mouth to savor the taste. She noticed for the first time an abstract picture on the wall, very much in the style of Helen Frankenthaler. Just like home. Rebecca's eyes were beginning to get heavy. If Tom didn't hurry up with his bathroom procedures, she would fall asleep before he could give her the traditional evening oral. Rebecca carefully opened the notebook in the middle, resolved to at least read a couple of pages. The first entry was dated back to late June, second half of the 00's.

Rebecca, turning the pages of Emma's diary, had to admit Emma was pretty rigorous about making entries, because she didn't fail to write in the diary, even if for just a few lines at a time. What was more, she was clearly a hopeless graphomaniac. It seemed that she recorded pretty much everything and pages and pages were devoted to musings about the most diverse subjects. She didn't shy away from politics, culture, history, music, movies... but kink was pretty much the dominant subject. She used an old fashioned fountain pen, judging from the elegantly drawn lines with differing strengths of line. Rebecca coursed through the elaborations on the stock market crisis and found the part of the notebook, dealing with the history of her late teenage years. She flew through the tearful episode of Severin leaving Emma to return to his wife and began to read right there — when Emma got to Berlin to begin her great summer adventure.

"... I have to find myself a place to stay, preferably one with a BDSM positive landowner, one who will not frown at me for having kinky guests from time to time. I'm going to call Cruella today. She seems to be the only person to be trusted. Thinking about Severin, how he betrayed me, not to mention Chiara! Cruella is not the looker, but she seems trustworthy and I'm determined not to get exploited ever again! Plus, she is very well connected in Berlin. I'm currently staying with people renting a room in Wilmersdorf, but I obviously need my own apartment to get some privacy. I won't downgrade my living

conditions... I always lived in large, stylish apartments and I have no intention of lowering my standards. Hopefully Cruella will have some recommendations."

Rebecca thought that young Emma was quite spoiled and skipped a few pages where Emma described the natural beauty of Berlin parks and historical architecture, together with eloquent descriptions of culinary pleasures in local restaurants and cafes, times enjoyed with all sorts of new acquaintances, men and women.

"Seems luck has struck! I'm moving to a new place tomorrow. Cruella stuck to her promise. There's a guy in Charlottenburg (that's the quarter I want to live in, one of the best of the Berlin neighborhoods!) who owns a block of flats - a submissive guy. Cruella said to me privately that he is on the quest to find himself a Mistress, but I thought, hey, so what? Perhaps I like him.

The three of us had a lunch together on the Ku'Damm Avenue. His name is Miguel, Spanish by the looks of it. Unlike most Spaniards I've met, he is not handsome - he is tall, but his figure isn't striking, his features are slightly irregular. Definitely not my type. He rambled about how he made a fortune in data mining and after that I ceased listening. Who cares? He clearly likes to boast and thinks he can impress me with his riches. I observed him and concluded that he tries to mask the lack of self-confidence, rather feebly, because I could see right through it.

He was smitten with me of course and agreed to rent me a very nice apartment on the second floor. He took me there this very day. The flat has high ceilings, a beautiful oriel window facing the square with large chestnuts - what an amazing view! And what's best, he has a BDSM studio in the cellar and he offered it to me for usage with no conditions at all! Oh, what parties I will throw... The place is splendid and the rent reasonable, I will be able to afford it comfortably with the funds from my parents. Not that I don't think that he gave me such a good offer because he hopes for something more... But that's not my problem now, is it?"

Rebecca thought that Emma's parents were quite incredible to support her financially even though she shunned them at the first opportunity, without as much as looking back. Rebecca was very curious about the story of Cruella, but Emma didn't mention it. Perhaps she missed it in the massive amount of text. Emma surely asked about it she remembered from the first glancing read! Rebecca moved several pages back. After Chiara made fool of Cruella and Emma back at the countryside party, she reportedly returned to Berlin to revenge herself. Rebecca scanned the pages until she arrived at the passage when Emma met with Cruella for a cup of tea in a local tea shop in Berlin Mitte. Almost a year had elapsed from the incident at the farm.

"... We met at Cruella's favorite place, a rather shabby cafe called Perdu (a French term for something past, like Proust's Recherche du Temps Perdu? Not my strongest suit, French) in an obscure side street. It had the feel of an opium den, with the dusty old pouffes and low hanging sleepy lamps. I half expected Sherlock to turn up, but mostly it was populated with nerdy students.

Cruella arrived late of course. She had not changed a single bit! Her frizzy hair flying around her head, her leather coat shapeless and waaaay too big, old tall boots with large buckles just like puss in boots and a crocheted tank top. Oh my... It takes some getting used to her! Unlike many other women, she seems blissfully oblivious to the fact that I look so much better than her. She is nothing like Mathilda! So many women seem hostile just because the other woman is better looking. Apparently, she has an inflated self-confidence. I considered the thought that she belongs to the category of people who delude themselves that they look way better than they do, persuading the others of it by their sheer force of confidence..."

The scathing analysis of Cruella's character continued, but

Rebecca looked up from reading. She knew that nowadays Emma would blush at this passage. Overall the teenage Emma seemed way more superfluous, concerned with other people's looks and much less lenient to the faults of others than her present self. Skipping another page or two with observations of Cruella's looks and style of clothing, she scanned the pages for the place where Chiara's name was mentioned again. Rebecca didn't enjoy the feeling of reading stuff she knew Emma would now be ashamed of. It didn't feel right. Then she read on.

"... When Cruella was leaving the farm cottage, she seemed very determined to make Chiara suffer for her insolence. After all, she double-crossed us both! I was so curious I could hardly contain it. She didn't notice or pretended not to and instead lead a polite chit chat on my satisfaction with staying in Berlin. I didn't beat around the bush though, and asked straight about it. Cruella seemed reluctant at first, clearly she was worried about my reaction. It took some convincing before she agreed to tell me all. What I learned shook me to the core."

Rebecca eyes opened wider, every trace of tiredness obliterated by the expectation. *"... Cruella explained to me that she eventually decided against taking revenge on Chiara. I just gaped at her as she was serenely sipping her jasmine tea. I recalled how livid she was when she was leaving the place after finding out what Chiara did... After the damn woman charged some of the slaves for the privilege to participate at our party without telling us. Not only I was shocked, I was disappointed! Chiara, who exploited me and made a lot of money off of me, deserved to be punished. At that moment I realized that I made a mistake to completely rely on Cruella in this respect. I expected her to live up to her name and make Chiara feel regret! And now here she was, serenely sipping tea, unconcerned that the cow Cruella wasn't held accountable for her immoral behavior. I could picture Chiara, stuck in her old ways, scheming to do a number on someone who deserved it. I told Cruella precisely that - in pretty direct manner. She was slightly taken aback by my sudden passionate outburst. She waved me down and explained what she actually meant. She's done something after all, only it wasn't the sort of revenge I envisioned."*

The bathroom door opened and the freshly shaved and showered slave Fuckboy walked out of the bathroom, his thick leather collar in place. No one would have guessed this well-built man was mere minutes ago the maid Priscilla - only a trace of black pencil on the lower eyelid betrayed him. Fuckboy soundlessly closed the door - he knew his Mistress hated how noisy he was - and dropped to his knees, crossing his arms behind his back, waiting next to the door. Rebecca looked at him and resolved to leave him there, kneeling. As Mistress Emma told her on one occasion, each slave should develop the skill to wait patiently in the corner until he is summoned. No Mistress should feel obliged to stop whatever she is doing just because her slave just arrived, ready for service. Rebecca gave him a sideways glance and instead of issuing a command, she returned to her reading.

"I thought Cruella's reasoning was interesting," Emma wrote, *"... so I will try to put it down here, word for word, as she said it. I might not remember everything, but I wanted to record it for future reference. Here goes what Cruella said to me: 'I thought of different scenarios - exposing Chiara to the community by shooting a secret video of her fucking her 'clients', sending an email to other Dommes to warn them against her. What was it that would make her sorry she was born? But with all the wicked ideas, I realized I'd mess up my karma pretty badly... I've known Chiara ever since she was in her early twenties. In her youth she was as enthusiastic and idealistic a Domme as myself. She loved Femdom for the sheer joy of the power exchange and wasn't in it for money. To other women she was sweet and supportive. What went wrong that she changed into such a bitch? I mused about it for quite some time before it struck me. I realized that all the changes to her character are to be attributed to one single change in her life and that was the key to all..."*

The page ended and Rebecca had to turn the page to learn what was the single thing in Chiara's life to make such a difference to her character. Rebecca paused and closed her eyes for a moment. When she breathed out, she clapped the notebook closed. In recent months she adopted the practice of resisting temptation and postponing pleasure whenever suitable opportunity arose. Postponing pleasure was touted as the most vital skill of the most successful people on this planet - in the media and in the books Rebecca read on personal growth. When she learned at the Club of the Dominant Wives, how essential it was as part of slave training, she decided to apply it to her slave as well, to strengthen character and will - each according to their role in the D/s. She instilled it in her slave Fuckboy, whom she teased and denied on every convenient occasion. Fuckboy never came without permission, an ejaculation accident didn't happen for many months... And she, she used the principles of denial to become a strong-willed woman just like Emma. She looked at the closed notebook, as if it was the most delicious cheese cake. Resisting temptation hurts so much, but it strengthens the character, she told herself... Moreover, there was a gratification at hand, superior to satisfied curiosity!

Rebecca snapped her fingers and pushed the duvet off of her, revealing her smoothly shaved bare legs and petite feet with perfectly manicured toes, each nail shining like a tiny red bead. Fuckboy, who was kneeling next to the bathroom door understood very well the power exchange aspect of why he was kneeling, being ignored, while his Mistress was reading and sipping wine.

Whenever he was kneeling in the corner, he used the time to entertain vivid fantasies of what was about to come, taunting his libido with every sensual detail. Usually, Mistress used him for oral before going to sleep. She rightfully called it the 'highlight of the evening'. He would faithfully serve her with his tongue even if he was dead tired. He would work to delight her body by offering his Mistress her favorite worship licks, flat tongue wide and slowly up, or sideways, sometimes flickering, his tongue erect and entering her temple, then soft caresses, sometimes gentle bites, and the use of his finger to finally tease a deep arousal from her G-spot. If it took her twenty minutes to come, his tongue would get as sore as his arms and chest would during a bench-press, but he would never ever give up, until she shook with orgasmic joy and he felt rewarded and a sense of purpose as a slave who had pleased his Mistress. He had a photo of her pussy on his slave phone to remind him of the most important purpose in his life - the complete satisfaction of his Mistress. Her pussy was every bit as beautiful as her feet, petite, shaved with some hair left in the shape of line. Thinking of his slave role, he managed to keep himself aroused and hard, ready for whatever his Mistress might fancy.

After cumming, Mistress Rebecca snapped her fingers to get his attention, and beckoned with her forefinger. Slave Fuckboy eagerly crawled on all fours towards her. There was a nice beige plush carpet next to the bed and he gratefully rested his knees on it, sore from kneeling on the cold floor. "Your maid initiation ceremony pleased me very well. C'mon you can claim your reward now..." Mistress Rebecca pressed her feet against his face. "My fragrant toes are waiting for you to bathe them. That's the first reward of this evening."

Although his mind was getting blank with all the blood leaving his swollen cock, Fuckboy still wondered what reward might come next - she said this is the first reward - there must be something else coming... His Mistress wasn't lavish with rewards and kept him strictly denied, so the reward surely would have to do with her own pleasure, not his. She shoved her toe into his mouth and made fucking motions. He eagerly sucked on it and made whimpering sounds that amused her. The smell of his Mistress' feet was a major turn on for him. It never failed to make him rock hard again. Unfortunately, his cock was still captured in the nasty pink prison.

"You don't need to say anything, I can read you like an open book, my boy," Rebecca smirked. "Your swelling cock looks pretty crammed in that pink prison... I can see how you fidget to relieve the discomfort."

She indeed saw right through him and he admired her ability to read his mind and his body language at all situations. His submission felt so right to have a Mistress who has this talent of 'clairvoyance'. "It's been a while..."

Rebecca took the fine necklace with the tiny key dangling on it, reflecting in the light as she took it off her neck. "I want to have some fun with my cock on your body. What's the use of it, if it is locked all of the time!" She expertly unlocked the key and took off the cage. Being locked for so long in chastity, a cock always needs a moment to recuperate and acclimate to its freedom. Rebecca left the ring, encompassing his cock and ball, in place.

"Now, masturbate," she commanded. "Yes, Mistress," breathed the Fuckboy. "But first, beg me for the selfish pleasure I am considering granting to you. If you please me with your begging, I may allow you to start stroking".
"Please Mistress Rebecca! It has been 3 weeks since my last ruined orgasm. I have tried to be obedient to you, working hard to anticipate your needs, serving you promptly when you call me. I worship you in my thoughts daily, trying to be good husband and a good slave for you... Please Mistress Rebecca, I beg you to allow me to cum before you on my knees as a sign of my devotion to your Femdom superiority."

"Well said slave, that was quite a plea! Your wish is granted. I will set the rhythm."

Rebecca took her riding crop and slapped lightly the palm of her hand, 1 - 2 - 3 - 4 - 1 - 2 - 3 - 4, she counted and he pumped accordingly. "Don't - slow - down - 4, 1 - 2 - 3 - 4,"

Rebecca slid down from the bed and began to stroll around him, still setting the rhythm with the riding crop. He was so horny, and was beginning to lag behind. "What do you think you're doing? Pump right, think of how Justin fucked you." Fuckboy was on the brink of cumming already, it didn't take much after all the weeks of denial and now he felt like he might ejaculate.

"Uh... Mistress... I'm afraid I might cum...," he said in a pleading tone. "You are strictly forbidden to cum, slave!" Fuckboy contorted his face with effort and returned to the pumping frequency his Mistress set with her crop.

"You know what I am thinking Fuckboy, I feel like having sex, real sex, you know? Not just the oral as usual."
"Yes Mistress..." He knew this was a game of will and that he would be punished if he accidentally ejaculated, or if he failed to observe the masturbation commands. He would be punished either way, but the punishment for an accidental ejaculation was always so much worse and painful. The mindfucking mention of regular sex completely derailed him. Fuckboy stopped pumping and collapsed with his face to the ground.

"I'm sorry Mistress, I cannot masturbate any longer!" Mistress Rebecca pretended to be annoyed by his lack of obedience.

"Well, well, well! I thought you might have better endurance?"
"I'm sorry, Mistress..." he whimpered. He was learning from Mistress Hannah's slave, who was always very expressive during BDSM scenes. He noticed Ladies of the Club enjoy that, so he also tried to make himself sound even more contrite and fearful. He could tell this effort was helping the D/s dynamics so he was not afraid to put in more drama.

"You should be... I was contemplating fucking you tonight, allowing you inside my vagina, but with this feeble performance I will have to lock you up again instead..." Fuckboy looked up. Was it just a game to tease him, or did she really intended to fuck him? Did he just ruin the chance he unconsciously desired all through the cuckolding and chastity, to feel her, penetrate her yet again?

"Can you even remember fucking me? When was the last time, slave? Well, your chance of cumming inside me, that unique opportunity is over. In fact, your time of selfish stroking enjoyment is over as well, come here now."

Fuckboy felt like he missed one number in the jackpot. Rebecca dragged him by the penis to the bathroom and showered his erect cock with cold water. It was enough to make his cock deflate like a punctured balloon.

"There now. No fucking for the slave cock. You slave cock needs to be locked up at all times, unless I fancy to enjoy a bit of fun sometime in the future. But don't hold your breath." She ordered him to put on the cage again, it was difficult for her to do so he had to assist with the procedure. The process of locking the key was, however, entirely in her hands.

Rebecca grabbed a leather leash hanging on a hook next to the bath tub, and attaching it to the D ring on his collar navigated him back to the bedroom.

"On Your Knees now." She opened the drawer in the chest by the wall and produced a thick sized dildo. While she was talking to him, she attached it to a strap on harness. "That's better. Now, who is it you serve? You will be reminded that you must pleasure me. I will help you with my cock. Do you think I should rely on you satisfying my own needs, when your cock is not ready to do

the job?"
Slave Fuckboy feebly tried to argue this point - of course he was ready for the job - but she cut him short and added a sharp face slap for insolence.

"Come here," she said and he came closer. Was he to put it on? "Yes, put it on. I want to fuck, but you will have no enjoyment, you will be just my fucking doll, just like dear Justin. His Mistress made him step into the harness and used the buckles to fit it tightly on his hips. She checked the tightness of the dildo. Even if she pulled on it, it didn't get further from his body than two centimeters. "Perfect. Now, lay down!" She unceremoniously pushed him onto the bed, the energy of the push sending the mattress into motion. She used the conveniently placed handcuffs, prepared by slave Cunt, to fix him to the bed. She climbed on top of him.

"I'm already wet from watching you masturbate, you bitch. I was expecting your throbbing cock inside me and now I won't tire myself with foreplay." Fuckboy was so turned on by Rebecca's harsh treatment, by the humiliating talk she spat at him, by the sternness in her voice, that when she mounted him and slowly sat onto the dildo, he was screaming inside with lust. She tweaked his nipples as his hands were restrained and the agony of thinking it could have been his cock that Mistress Rebecca was riding, was the worst torture and the most intense humiliation imaginable. She was sighing, masturbating her clit with her hand as she fucked the dildo. She took off her blouse and removed her bra and he watched her swaying boobs as she coiled and glided up and down on the dildo. She was enjoying it, putting in all her sensuality and sex-appeal. He knew she was enjoying it so much and making it even more alluring show for him, because his cock wasn't in her, the pleasure was not his, it was hers and hers only.

Rebecca, who was so proficient in guessing his thoughts,

laughed. That scathing, sarcastic laugh that made him more a slave. "Oh, look at my cuckold Fuckboy, the hope rekindled and shattered again... Hmm... does it feel good?... no?... it feels so good to me, oooh so good... Do you think that anything you do can get you a fuck with me again? Forget about it!"

She increased the speed of her fucking and her voice was short of breath. "You are just a slave, a whore maid at best." She played with her nipples and slowed down again, taking the dildo possessively into her vagina, letting it glide as deep as it would go. ".. I have other lovers, who can have me.. who want me... Real men, not such a whimpering sissy maid... Next time I will have you lay under this bed when my lover fucks me, so that you can hear how it sounds when I'm getting laid by some Alpha Male, not a sissy slave like you."

"Yes, Mistress, I'm not a lover worthy of you, I'm just your lowly sissy slave... a beta to all your alpha lovers!"

Upon hearing those words of her cuckold slave's devotion, his Mistress stopped speaking. She stated masturbating herself with her hand, still fucking her slave's strap on cock instead of his real penis. All that, while listening to her thoughts and his words pushed her over the top... and Rebecca finally exploded in the shivering quiver of a loud satisfying orgasm.

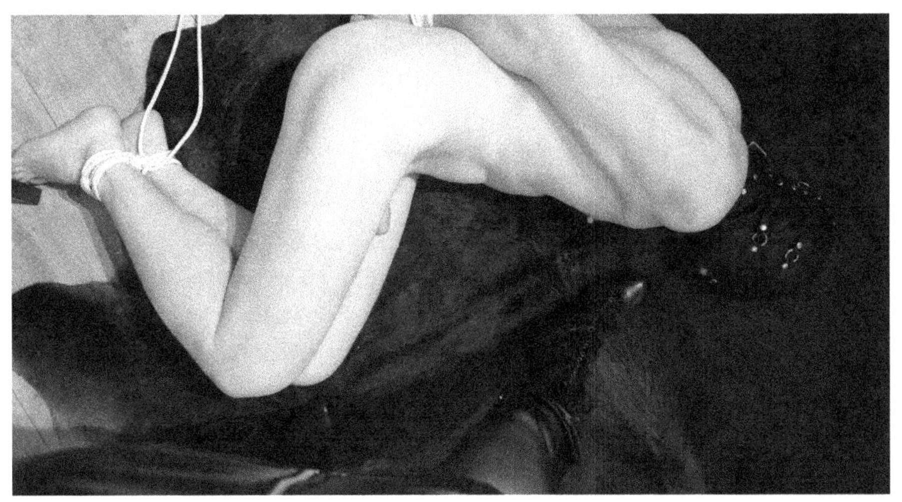

CHAPTER 13

2016

It was a glorious morning. The sun was already far above the Frauenkirche, claiming superiority over the landscape and bathing the interior of the spacious apartment with optimistic light. The slaves rose early to prepare the breakfast for their Mistresses.

Emma, spread wide on the queen-sized bed, was dreaming about amazing Vermont maple syrup covered pancakes that smelled so good her mouth began to water in her sleep. Emma smiled with her eyes still closed when she came round and realized, that the smell wasn't just the fabric of her sweet dreams. It was real!

The tireless endeavor to turn her slave Cunt into a pancake-proficient cook, able to conjuring up the most delicious, translucent pancakes, was finally coming to fruition. Emma was sleeping naked, which was her preference in the warm, summer months, and lazily stretched herself, resolved to relish the pleasant feeling of waking slowly from a refreshing sleep, but then she envisioned the thin pancakes with cream, strawberries, and that wonderful maple syrup. She could hear the slaves taking plates out of the cupboard. It would be a sacrilege to let the pancakes turn cold...

She dropped her feet to the side of the bed, where her heeled slippers waited, neatly arranged by slave Cunt so that she could slip into them effortlessly. She stood up and was totally unconcerned that with binoculars her statuesque naked figure could be easily seen through the large window. So be it - Emma was not ashamed of her figure, and even though she had two children, her figure was as perfect as decade ago. She always modestly waved down compliments, thanking the genetics rather than any restraint in eating or exercise.

Emma grabbed her favorite pink dressing gown that she had bought on her trip to Rome and putting it on, she walked out of the room. At precisely the same moment Hannah walked out of her room.

"Is it just me, or does something smell yummy?"
Emma grabbed her by the hand. "No, dear, these are the most amazing pancakes, the best you ever had! They smell so divine they even found their way into my dreams!"

Their slaves welcomed them with a kiss on their naked toes peeping out of their elegant home slippers.

Rebecca had awoken from her sleep much earlier, only to find that Tom was already up, preparing himself to get ready for the morning service in the bathroom. She heard the metal parts of his handcuffs clatter on the tile floor. Rebecca reached for Emma's diary on the bedside table. It was not yet half past six, they went to bed at two o'clock and both Emma and Hannah would undoubtedly sleep in to make up for the late night. Perfect time to move forward in Emma's story! She began reading where she ended the previous day, in the middle of the dialogue of Emma and Cruella:

"'You are trying to find excuses for Chiara! Sorry Cruella, but just for the sake of old acquaintance you decided to let her go away with her abominable behavior?!' I almost yelled and people in the cafe started to notice me... whispering to each other. 'Calm down, Emma, wait to hear the rest of it.' I shut up, but I listened with my brows knitted, and stirred my tea so violently, it was splashing around my cup. I was angry. Cruella continued, speaking faster than usual, probably afraid I might go ballistic. 'I thought to myself, there is one thing in Chiara's life that if removed, might get back the Chiara I used to know. If I made her see some sense and mend her ways, wouldn't it be preferable than aggressive revenge? The revenge might give you and me the instant satisfaction, but it would change nothing. Chiara would probably continue to be the insufferable bitch she is...' "

Tom walked out of the bathroom. He couldn't help but notice, how gorgeous his wife looked in the morning, the diary perched on her knees, her night gown was enticingly parted on her chest. The term 'beauty sleep' must have been invented for her personally. She looked so fresh and well-rested! He loved her without make up. She looked less stern without her eyes framed with black line, sort of kinder, but it was quite on the contrary. In the morning, her dominant batteries were charged. While she was lenient in the evening, in the morning she was again the demanding and stern Mistress he both loved and was terrified of.

"Mistress, I'm sorry, but I woke up again with an erection. Of

course the cage took care of it, but I have to report that.
 "Yes you do! It's no wonder you did have a morning wood, after all that happened the previous day!"

"You are a most generous, Mistress..."

"Well, I didn't say that you are going to be spared the punishment, now did I?"

"No, Mistress..."

"But I will ask Mistress Hannah to administer it, she is always so pleased to take care of it."
Fuckboy felt an intense surge of thrill and excited panic at the same time. Mistress Hannah was very sexy, but her hand was heavy, and she was completely merciless.

Rebecca pulled him closer by his hair. "Time for your licking practice - the weekend regime applies - I'm sure other Ladies are still fast asleep, so we have plenty of time."

Fuckboy dived down and lovingly looked at Mistress' trimmed pubic hair and the beautiful pussy when she spread her legs. His Mistress adored long oral practice and they practiced Saturdays, Sundays and holidays, until his licking endurance greatly improved. The slave had to lick his Mistress when she was watching TV or reading. With her mind occupied, the climax came after much longer time and the slave could improve his licking endurance. She was tempted, as always, to close her eyes and let her mind conjure up sexy fantasies to cum, but she reminded herself of the great sensation of seemingly endless cunilingus. She breathed contentedly, and when he began flicking his tongue she opened the notebook again. It took some effort to refocus on the story, but she read on.

"I still had no clue what she was talking about. ' What do you mean?

You make it sound like she is under a curse and if you disenchant her, she will be her former self? Doesn't make sense to me.' Cruella sprinkled cinnamon on top of her latte. 'That's because you still don't get it. Do you remember Marcus?' Of course I remembered. 'You mean Chiara's husband?' 'The very one, yes.' 'Sure, when I was staying at their place, I thought him rather creepy. I also thought, even though I cannot prove it, he was spying on me when I was bathing. His eyes seemed to follow me everywhere. Gave me creeps.' Cruella gave a sip of her latte, but the coffee was too hot, so she set it on table again. 'Well, I realized that it is him, who made such a difference to her behavior, that he is playing her like a violin.' 'Hang on, are you trying to tell me that Marcus is to blame that she is money thirsty bitch, who exploits her friends for her own material gain? Isn't this a bit far-fetched?' Cruella smiled. 'You need to understand the whole story to see my point.' I guess I rolled my eyes at that point. This sounded like she was about to come up with very long and tiresome story, but I braced myself. 'Did you know, that Chiara's dad died when she was little?' I didn't, but it didn't make any difference to me, anyway. What was it to me, what family did Chiara grew up in... 'Doesn't make me feel compassionate, sorry.' I retorted. 'You don't need to be, I just want you to understand her personality.' I shrugged, like I couldn't care less, but listened."

Rebecca could hear shuffling of feet in the next room and Emma's mischievous laughter. She was probably up and about to perform her morning rituals on her slave - the preventative caning discipline and piss drinking. She still had a bit of time... Fuckboy never served her with oral service for shorter time stretches than half an hour and she was resolved not to break this rule. Rebecca could feel her slave slowing down.

"Don't slow down, I'm not done with you yet. You are licking your Mistress for barely fifteen minutes!" The licking resumed and Rebecca read on:

"'What followed was an all too common scenario. Her mother

remarried, had another child and she and Chiara's step dad paid her very little attention. The child from the previous marriage began to feel unwanted and unloved. The parents failed miserably to provide her with love she needed. With the love that every child needs! As a result, Chiara, when she grew up, was always thirsty for love and appreciation. And all that resulted into another pretty typical thing. She is magnetically attracted to men who exploit her. Inherently, she doesn't feel worthy of love and believes that love is conditional. She thinks that she must earn it. Marcus instinctively felt her weakness and played her to achieve his own ends. He has the uncanny talent to make her do whatever he wants! In the beginning, he was her slave, but soon he realized that she was far too anxious to make him happy and she was endlessly needy for his love and approval. Eventually, the whole dynamics shifted and within a few years he turned her into a hen, laying golden eggs. He doesn't work at all, he uses her to make the money for their household. She is under immense pressure to provide for the family and she does it by doing paid Femdom sessions. She is anxious that if she did not bring enough money, he might leave her...' I finally dropped the pose of unconcerned disinterest. 'Okay, I admit this is getting interesting. But what is it you wanna do about it?' Cruella seemed pleased that I finally was coming around to her. 'Well, the plan is already unfolding, but you surely can lay your stealthy hand to the job!' "

Another fifteen minutes elapsed and clinking of teacups and plates reminded Rebecca, that it was high time to get out of the bed and join the others at breakfast, but of course she couldn't miss her morning orgasm! Rebecca closed the notebook, she could ask Emma about the rest of the story later.

"Slave, time for the sweet finale! I will tell you about the wonderful date with my lover last week.' 'Yes Mistress, please!' Fuckboy breathed, he knew how Rebecca relished teasing him about her lovers. She always saved her mind-boggling dirty talk for occasions like that. She was cruel to his pride in describing it, but he cherished each detail of Rebecca's cuckolding adventures.

It was the matrix of his erotic fantasies and her words that resonated in his head on sleepless nights, when he desired nothing more, but to break free from his metal cage and masturbate violently.

"You saw Horst in the gym? Admit it, yes? What an athletic body he has! Oh, he is so sexy... Rebecca began to fondle her nipples. 'It felt so good when he pressed his firm body against mine in the locker room..." Fuckboy envisioned how they ripped the clothes off their bodies, how his Mistress willingly yielded to this other man's advances, how he shoved his tongue into her mouth, something he imagined to be the first penetrative act before he claimed her with his cock. Rebecca pressed her eyelids closer together and bit her lip, as she thought the same thoughts.

Rebecca teased Tom, her voice getting lower: "... We were all sweaty after exercise session together. He then snuck in the empty female locker room and jammed the door tight so no one could get in. Looking at me with his blue eyes, he pleaded that I drove him insane with my sexual alure. Then, with his muscles pumped and hard, he ripped my shirt open and sucked my nipples. I never was so attracted to a man in my life. He pinned me against the lockers, we were making out so passionately!"

Rebecca began to move her pelvis against Fuckboy's tongue. Fuckboy only saw his wives' boobs getting exposed for the pleasure of another male. "I dived down and pulled the boxers to his ankles. I couldn't wait to see and admire his glorious cock. His cock is so big too, nothing like yours! I knelt. I wanted to suck it."

Fuckboy's tongue already felt like it wasn't his anymore, but he increased the speed, willing it to keep going to give his Mistress her deserved pleasure.

".. He teased my pussy with his fingers and it was oozing wet. He moistened the head of his cock with my juices as he massaged my clit, but wouldn't penetrate me. I couldn't stand the desire, so I took him into my mouth. When I tasted my own juices, mingling with his precum, I knew there was nothing more important in the world than to satisfy him. I deep-throated him and he coiled my ponytail around his hand to fix my head and do whatever he wanted with it. I was his fuck toy, his face fuck, my eyes watered from gagging on his cock... mascara was running... saliva was dripping. His large cock almost suffocated me. When he let go, I pleaded with him to finally have me. He was making me desperate with lust to be fucked... He just smirked at my desperate longing for his cock. He said 'Only if you say: Please Master fuck me like a whore.' I did! I repeated it over and over. "I had to beg, beg him to fuck me!" Then Horst took hold of me, pushed my legs wide apart, and impaled me with his thick stone-hard cock."

Rebecca was breathing harder now, she grabbed Fuckboy's hair and began to move her pelvis against his mouth as she was nearing to her orgasm. "Oh... Horst fucking me was out of this world. Each thrust he pounded against me was powerful and oh so deep."

Rebecca knew how horny this made her slave Tom feel and she relished her power to humiliate him. "Lick faster, you little cuckold...!" He flicked faster. "I only fuck real men, not sissy slaves like you, you will never feel my pussy around your cock, you will just lick the semen of other Alpha males oozing from my pussy." Fuckboy whimpered with lust. Pushed by erotic pleasure, over the edge of tease, Rebecca climaxed so loudly, everyone in the apartment must have heard.

"Nice to know you are enjoying yourselves. You look radiant, Rebecca," said Emma, who was beaming, as her slave Cunt was putting a cloth napkin on her lap.

Rebecca blushed slightly. "This is what good old oral pussy worship can do to your complexion." Fuckboy, who arrived few steps behind his wife in his slave uniform, was secretly proud. Rebecca accepted the compliment with gracious airs and the Ladies sat to the table to let themselves be waited upon by their slave husbands.

"Did you have the opportunity to do some reading?" Emma asked, sitting down and ordering the pancakes she was looking forward to. She was so proud, as she watched her slave confidently serve the pancakes, that were flawless - perfectly round, thin and without traces of burn, or tear.

"Yesterday, I ended up at the passage where you described what Cruella said about her revenge on Chiara. I decided to exercise the strength of will, so I shut the diary closed before learning what was the single influence in Chiara's life that was responsible for her change to complete assho.. Sorry, I mean the influence which made her change so much." Rebecca blushed, she didn't like using profanities, but being surrounded predominantly by males at work, sometimes it slipped with her. "But I did some reading in the morning too and learned about Marcus... So far I don't know what Cruella decided to do about him."

Emma smiled as much as her full mouth of pancakes allowed. "Hmph," she covered her mouth. "Sorry." She gulped and wiped her mouth with a cloth napkin. Rebecca looked down on her plate, where two pairs of absolutely perfect pancakes smiled at her. She hesitated to run her knife through the pancake, it looked so good it was a pity to ruin it. "It had occurred to me that she was in her husband's pocket, judging from what you said earlier."

Emma nodded. "Oh yes. I have to admit I have never encountered a woman, let alone a dominant one, who would be so anxious to please her husband. Previously, when I had stayed in their apartment, I noticed that there wasn't a single movement, a single look, that she would do without his approval. It was surprisingly absurd, considering she was well established within the community as a Domme. But you can ask all the others in the evening who were there."

Slave Fuckboy looked up. Emma noticed Fuckboy's inquiring look and distractedly dropped her fork. Mistress Hannah cleared her throat. Fuckboy thought it pretty weird, especially because they hastily changed the subject. This only made his resolution that they are plotting against him, stronger. Who were 'the others'?

Emma, more careful about what she would let slip, waited until all the slaves were in the kitchen. "You will surely wonder what it was that Cruella came up with. What's more, you will meet a person that could help to shed light on the whole story."

"Who is it?" wondered Rebecca.

"Wait to see!" Emma winked at her. "I won't tell you more right now. I don't want to spoil the fun." Rebecca complained, but to no avail, Emma remained adamant.

"Well, at least you could tell me how it went with Miguel." Emma ordered a second of the fantastic pancakes. "I most surely can! I moved in and before I unpacked, Miguel was there, knocking on my door. It felt like he was there, every minute of every day, hovering around me like a fly around an apple tart. We dined together in fancy restaurants, visited kinky shops together, he invited me to admire his collection of sport cars... He took me to his BDSM cellar studio, reminding me that I could use it in any way I liked. Still, he was too shy to offer himself to me as a slave. He was convenient, because the more I knew him, the more unacceptable he was to me with his inflated sense of self, his bragging. But of course I found his help rather useful, so I kept our connection afloat."

"That was the time when we met for the first time, Emma." Hannah noted. "Right! I was lucky to meet you, I guess I can thank your influence for not sinking me into the seedy underbelly of the BDSM scene."

"Well, but it took you quite a while to see sense in it... Think of your first months in Berlin, what you were doing..." "What? What did Emma do?" Rebecca asked, looking from Hannah to Emma and back again.

Emma waved her hand "Oh, well... I was young."

"Don't try to downplay it Emma, tell it all to Rebecca as it was, it will do you good to put some ashes of penitence on your head in front of other Ladies."

Emma hanged her head. "Yes Ma'am, but please, you start."

"I will. Emma and I met at a fetish party of a tattoo studio... Have you been to one yourself, Rebecca?" Rebecca shook her head. "Well, you can guess how that looks. People with all sorts of body modifications, covered head to toe with tattoos, with forked tongues, large gaping holes in their earlobes, or horns, all mingling with latex-clad fetishists and heavily made-up divas. And then there was Emma in her sexy red latex dress, being carried in a specially designed chair by four slaves. I admit I thought her intolerably vain and proud."

"Yeah, I turned up with my five house slaves... I didn't know a soul in there, but I behaved like I ruled the game. I didn't care about the rules, I didn't bother to make friends, I kept to myself and associated with subs only. I was a pain in the ass to the community." Emma mused.

"Can you wonder? Ladies universally hated you, because you were vain and you dissociated from them." Hannah said.

Emma smiled gently. "Well, being nineteen at that time I gained incredible traction because of my dominant youthful attraction. I had just created my first website where I rambled on about Femdom. My mailbox was instantly flooded with hundreds and hundreds of messages each day... Subs flocked to me, I was like a fox in a hen house of the Berlin scene, to some Dommes. I didn't mean any harm, but quite a number of slaves, especially the low-quality ones just ditched their Mistresses to serve me. I didn't think I needed to bother about other Dommes."

Rebecca gaped. "Wow, that doesn't sound like you at all". Emma shrugged. "We all need to start somewhere. I started as vain, reckless and completely uninterested in the feelings of others. If I'm to be completely honest, I thought that other Dommes essentially stood in my way to achieve the ultimate world rule of all men." Rebecca laughed incredulously but then her face changed when Emma didn't laugh along.

"No, I am joking," Emma said when she noticed how shocked Rebecca looks. "But... actually I'm not joking?" she said sheepishly. "I really wanted all males to serve me and me only! My highly moral character and Domme friendliness philosophy took a number of years to form."

"Not that I would defend you, because you behaved like complete bitch... but in a sense you just followed the pattern of many Dommes. As we know, Dominant women of course tend to be very independent and it takes a lot of concentrated effort on their part to form any friendships with other Dommes... It is an exception rather than a rule. We are all very strong personalities, individualists, and do not tend to seek approval of others like weak people do."

Rebecca looked derailed and frowned slightly. "That's so weird - in absolute contrast to my own experience with you all and the Club! You were giving me such a helping hand from the very beginning and I never, for a second felt like we wouldn't have the most amazing relationship with one another."

Emma nodded smugly. "Well, I can honestly say that our Club is one of a kind. I guess you could count such coherent, safe Domme clubs on the fingers of one hand."

"Hang on, did you actually say that you had five house slaves? Like, staying with you? At home?" Rebecca wondered.

Emma looked at her innocently. "Would you expect anything less from me? You know that I tend to overdo everything, it is my personality feature to try and try everything in the most eccentric way... I created my first slave ring and it was fascinating, living like a Princess with the slaves to wait upon me in all areas of life... But that was not enough for the fanatic young me! Many slaves who were not capable of serving me 24/7 were so eager to serve me, but I had to refuse them in dozens. It was then I realized that subs are more than willing to pay to serve me. I soon found myself showered with money and certainly wasn't moral enough to refuse. Mind you, I was still a teenager, I found myself for the first time in my life with money I didn't even know what to do with. I received many gifts - expensive furs, perfumes, vouchers for expensive lingerie shops, you name it. I flaunted all the money at extravagant restaurants and to buy designer goods... Ahhh.. I'm quite ashamed when I think of it. But the world belongs to the young, attractive Domme."

"That must have left Miguel quite disillusioned... He was alright with you living with other slaves?" Rebecca wondered. Emma accepted freshly pressed orange juice from Hannah's slave, giving him a radiant smile.

"I must admit that at the time I was very little concerned about the feelings of others. I was doing my best to piss off many, many people. Miguel was attracted to me like a moth to a light, but he obviously hated all the slaves that hung around me. In some twisted way it humiliated him and he enjoyed it against his better judgment. I used my superpower - empathy - to read him. I soon made him one of my slave herd, because I realized he might easily lose his interest and drive me away. I didn't like the idea of leaving the magnificent apartment and the possibilities of the BDSM dungeon."

"Wow, again, this doesn't sound like you at all."

"That's why I'm telling you, I want you to understand my life story and this is, unfortunately a part of it. Somehow I derived psychological gratification from seeing Miguel suffer. You know what they say - if you find your soulmate, that person draws the best out of you. In the case of Miguel I can easily say that he drew the absolute worst out of me. It is difficult to explain, but I hated him for his character features, which in many ways were so much like my own. His haughtiness, boastful behavior... I realized much later in life that I despised him so much, because these were my characteristics too and he mirrored them. I didn't like the reflection a single bit! In despising him I was in a subconscious way, despising myself. I was torturing and treating him so badly, yet he always bounced back! That made me to treat him even worse. I was devising intricate ways to make him suffer. I'm endlessly ashamed of it now, because I was incredibly cruel towards him." Emma sighed. "Oh, well. He's fine now. Even though I guess he still hopes against hope that one day we end up together. As a proper sub he is endlessly loyal to me, despite my abhorrent behavior."

"But at that point you had to start at the university, right?"

Rebecca asked.

"Quite right." I admit that when the school studies started I took it very seriously. What annoyed me at the high school - the necessity to sit there for hours on end, didn't apply here. I was free to go to the classes or not to go and it was entirely up to my own decision. The factor of freedom was much better suited to my independent character. I ended up attending all classes and taking up the voluntary ones.

"Wait, how could you attend university and juggle it all with dominating five slaves?" Rebecca wondered. Emma neatly folded the napkin and set it to the side of her plate. "Of course this made my time much more precious. Can you imagine how time consuming is to supervise five slaves? Obviously, they need attention and a semblance of interest from their dominant. By taking five slaves I failed to realize it was a big responsibility."

"I didn't want to say that myself, but it is utter madness indeed. It is quite enough to dedicate the time to train one house slave. It makes no sense to have so many at home." Hannah observed.

"Right. I found myself unable to keep all five of the slaves! I just ditched three of them and kept two. I was not very sensitive about it and of course they were shattered to the core. I didn't even bother to come up with a feeble excuse, I just got rid of them."

"Seems that you were getting some sense?" Rebecca asked carefully.

"Of course she didn't..." Hannah smirked.

"Well, my wild years were not over yet." Emma admitted.

"I turned twenty and still attended all the fetish parties, but

I began to think of traveling abroad to study. I had my eyes on England... I loved good old England as I envisioned it based on Sherlock Holmes books, sisters Brontë and Jane Austen. I pursued a scholarship to travel to one of the top-tier English universities. And then it happened - the ominous letter arrived".

"What letter?" Rebecca asked.

"A letter - a slap to the face that marked the end of the wildest era of my Femdom life." Emma said enigmatically.

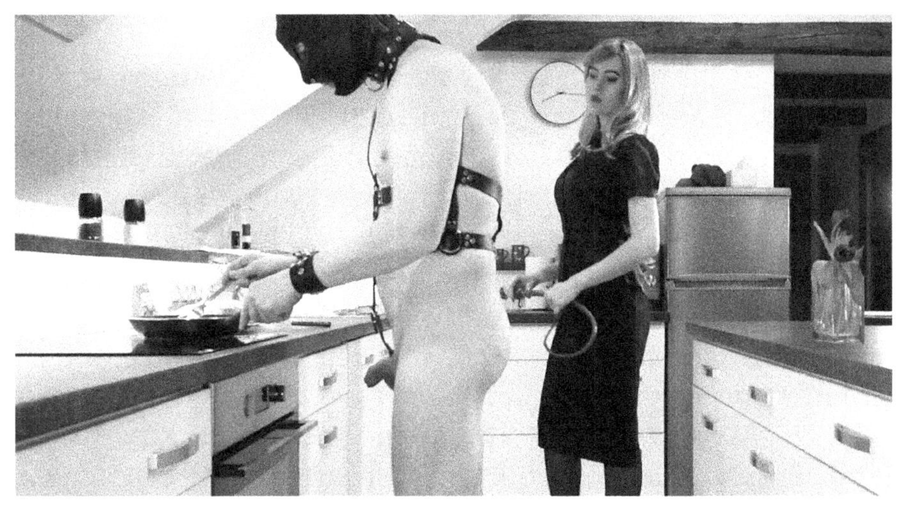

CHAPTER 14

2016

The Ladies, Emma, Hannah and Rebecca arrived on foot to the court of the sumptuously decorated Zwinger Palace of Dresden. It was within walking distance of their apartment and in the present weather it made for a very nice walk in the historical center. The spring was at its most glorious, long flowerbeds of tulips of bright colors stretched in all directions like colorful dragons at a Chinese festival. Entering the ground floor of the side wing, the Ladies headed to visit the renowned exhibition of applied arts.

"I'm glad you joined me. I think everyone coming to Dresden should visit the renowned art collection of August the Strong, containing some of the most audacious and extravagant treasures of the flamboyant eighteenth century," Emma said in the tone of a snobbish art connoisseur. "But I have something very special to show you here, I hope you won't get discouraged by a bit of history before I show you what I want to show you."

"Well, the baroque is bit too decorative for me, but a bit of history cannot hurt and we need to give our slaves a bit of time to prepare the picnic for us," Rebecca replied as they paid entrance fee and strolled into the gallery.

"Yeah, I know, you like better the abstract penises," said Emma merrily, referring to the replica of 'Princess X' Rebecca and Tom had in the hall of their home.

"Ah, well, there are a number of ways to interpret Brancusi."

"Yeah, sure. I know the history of that work of art, but why don't you admit you like cock?" Emma quipped and Rebecca could think of nothing to contradict that, so they entered in and soon they were consumed by the universe of the grandiose, dramatic and pathos-filled art of the baroque period.

Walking between the showcased exhibits, the precious gems set in most ostentatious jewelry, vessels, chinaware and diminutive gold-ladden marble sculptures, Emma arrived to the artifact she was looking for and read the inscription again to refresh her memory.

Meanwhile, Hannah studied a 'Rape of Proserpine', made of ivory, commenting loudly: "Look at all those naked couples, the perverts were using the excuse of mythology to elicit forbidden thoughts and kindle the erotic desire."

"Wait till you see this! Come here!" Emma called and the other two Ladies gathered around Emma, who squatted next to a tiny sculpture, a composition that, at first, didn't make sense to them.

"What...?"

"Let me introduce to you 'Aristotle and his wife'. This is the special thing I wanted you to see!" Emma explained. Both Ladies bowed down to squint at the tiny thing.

"... is she actually sitting on his back?" Rebecca wondered.
"... and she is actually flogging him with a cat o'nine tails!" Hannah laughed, pointing at the minuscule details of the marble, embellished with gold.

"I can imagine that there were subs three hundred years ago too... One of them probably made that," Rebecca suggested.

"It could be, or perhaps the commissioner? I guess you could claim that it has a parable potential. It could be used to demonstrate how bad it is when women rule their husbands," Emma smirked. She was pleased to find out both her friends thought the tiny thing every bit as amusing as she did.

"Well, that's probably the first and the last Femdom themed sculpture in this collection, so feel free to examine the rest at your own pace and then we can go for a picnic. I'm sure our boys have it all set up by now."

After a hundredth super fascinating and unique vessel made out of sea shell or rhinoceros horn, Rebecca was becoming bored. Hannah, on the other hand, enthusiastically jumped from one exhibit to another.

Rebecca cornered Emma, who had just paused to enjoy the fresh air and the view from the opened window, from which a pleasant spring air flew, bringing in the smell of hyacinths that were blooming on the flowerbeds around the palace.

"Emma, what was in that letter you told me about in the morning? You know what I mean - the one you said marked the end of your wild Femdom year."

"Oh, well... It is an Agatha Christie sort of story. So very many suspects and each and every one has a guilty conscience. It was almost impossible to sort out who actually did it..."

"Did what? Why are you always just giving hints and let me wonder? Why don't you tell me right away? It seems you enjoy taunting me!" Rebecca said, frustrated.

"Well, I do enjoy taunting you. It makes me more interesting in your eyes, doesn't it? I enjoy being interesting," Emma laughed, but Rebecca didn't seem too much amused.

"Alright, alright. The letter - the damn letter I should rather say - brought a lot of sleepless nights to me, but also helped me to realize that I cannot get away with behaving like a jerk. The letter was a blackmail! It arrive by post in a plain envelope without a return address. It was written by hand and it said just this:

'I know what you are and I will tell at the uni.'

"Oh no... !" Rebecca said.

Emma nodded gravely. "Oh yes."

Emma smiled at two elderly museum visitors and waited for them to pass before continuing. "I was pretty serious about my schooling and I certainly didn't want the situation from my high school to repeat. What if they expelled me? I didn't want to risk that! But there was nothing more, no conditions, nothing.

I turned the paper around, looked into the envelope over and over, but there was nothing that would suggest what the person wanted. I was left to wait to see if another letter arrived. All the time I was checking my phone and waiting for some representative of the university to call me and inform me that they will expel me for my perverse behavior."

"Can they actually do that?" Rebecca wondered.
"Not sure, back then the LGBTQ didn't have such an unshakable position as today. But you can imagine how terrified I was by the possibility. Also I had a superb reputation as a bright student with great future with stellar career prospects. I also wanted the scholarship to go to England. I wanted it so bad! And now all that was in jeopardy. I was stressed, worried. The week before another letter arrived belonged to the most horrific in my life."

"Have you had any idea who the blackmailer might be?"

"Oh well, as I already told you. I behaved despicably in the year before receiving this letter. It might have been anyone whom I irritated by my selfish behavior... Or someone else entirely."

"Surely you had your suspicions," Rebecca suggested. Emma turned from the window and she was frowning.

"Oh yes, I did! And I acted on that suspicion immediately."

CHAPTER 15

2016

It was late in the afternoon. Sissy Priscilla was kneeling at the feet of Mistress Rebecca, chilling after the intense drill of sissy skills that ensued after they returned from the picnic in the park. Tom pushed his boundaries again and felt proud to move closer to his Mistress' goal to turn him into a maid who would look, walk and conduct herself as the ultimate sissy servant. The last few days had been a very interesting Femdom experience for Tom, to a large degree thanks to Mistress Hannah, who was seasoned at sissy training and didn't regret the effort to help Rebecca. Tomorrow morning they were supposed to return to Berlin and he was already sorry to change the kink universe that was drawing him in and making him more and more regretful to leave each time he entered it.

Tom found himself increasingly fantasizing about the 24/7 slavery with his smart, successful wife ruling him around the clock and him staying at home as her servant and slave. He could easily envision the life they would have. He would take care she was pampered like a queen, her every need taken care of and he, her worm, would spend every minute of his day thinking of her and her comfort. He would live off the leftovers, or eat whatever she chose to throw off the table while eating. He would serve her so that she wouldn't have to lift a finger around the house. Whenever she'd return from work, he would massage her whole body and help her relax, give her long, long oral. On the evenings when her girlfriends would turn up for a glass of wine or a party, he would morph into Priscilla, the perfectly trained maid, who would patter around on her stilettos to freshen up Ladies' drinks, serve dishes and - hopefully - get played with a bit by his Mistress' more adventurous female friends. So far, with the present income of their household, it was just a dream - but if their investment strategies worked as expected, perhaps in the not too distant future, this vision might come to fruition. The mere idea gave him so much satisfaction it occupied his thoughts every time he was going to sleep and most mornings as the first thing that emerged on his mind with the first sun rays.

When they returned from the picnic, Rebecca issued a command that Tom put on his complete maid costume again. Tom was grateful that they would use the last evening to improve him under the stern guidance of Mistress Hannah. Originally, the Ladies planned to venture out clubbing, but after the eventful day they felt like chilling in, instead. Priscilla slipped into her maid uniform, rolled up her net stockings. Charlotte, with the long fake nails, was helping her to put on make up and a wig. For at least twenty minutes she danced around Priscilla with her brushes. When she was done, Tom almost couldn't recognize himself in the mirror. He blinked a few times, getting used to the feeling of having thick layers of mascara on his lashes and the sticky feeling on his mouth from the lip gloss. The make up that made him unrecognizable, was helping him to make the switch to his sissy identity. The more he was practicing, the easier the transition was becoming.

Together with the ability to feel into her sissy role almost instantaneously, Priscilla improved her walking in high heels. She didn't look so clumsy and 'square' anymore. She learned to sway her hips and move her hands elegantly. That day Priscilla was instructed how to carry a tray, how to curtsy, serve drinks and refreshments without the clumsy awkwardness. Throughout the training she was having an anal plug in, fixed with a tight, restrictive thong to stay in place.

But now, it was over! Evening was slowly approaching and the Ladies agreed they were tired, ready for early bed. Tom was sorry to see the Femdom adventure end. He tried to shun the intrusive thought that the day after he would be yet again stuck at work, with just his memories of the perfect few days to support him through the dull tasks of his tedious job. He was sent into the kitchen to wash the dishes, but then, there was a knock on the door. He froze in his spot, listening. Mistress Emma answered the door and he could hear a hubbub of voices.

CHAPTER 16

2008

Two girls in their twenties, best friends by the looks of it, were strolling among the flowerbeds at the Ku'damm. They enjoyed both looking at others and being looked at. It was obvious to the keen eye that they both made quite an effort to look good on that particular May day. The weather warranted minimalist clothing and so the blond teenager sported mini shorts with a twist crop tank and the brunette, whose middle section was on the heavier side of slim, didn't shy away from a mini skirt that exposed her long slim legs, she was so proud of.

"... so will I also see one of your.. You know what I mean... one of the... slaves?" she mouthed the last word as if she just tasted something and couldn't decide whether is was good or disgusting.

"I don't know Mathilda, I guess that it is not for everyone." Emma drew in her voice and pretended to stare into the show window of a fancy boutique. "I think that this will be my next holy grail... look at those sleeves..." Mathilda didn't listen.

"Come on, you know I like to try new things!" she insisted and grabbed Emma under arm. Emma looked at her, weighing the options.

"You are too vanilla for that."

Mathilda was puzzled. "I'm what?"

"Well, a Muggle. Non-magical creature," Emma winked.

This struck Mathilda, she always wanted to into the middle of the action and hated to be left out. "How can you be so sure?"

"I know you, right?" Emma brushed her back in a condescending gesture. She felt Mathilda's bra that was too tight around her back and caused her back to form fat folds. It made her sick and she removed her hand immediately.

"Well, you don't. I think there is a kinky side to me!" Mathilda said indignantly.

"Well, in that case, I might take you with me. I have a session with one of my particular favorites in an hour or so."

"Alright! Is he good looking?"

"You bet! Your type in fact - tall, dark and handsome."

"Okaaay!" Mathilda clapped her hands enthusiastically.

Emma smiled back at her and thought, how easy it was to play Mathilda. Didn't she realize that she, Emma, knew it was Mathilda who humiliated her in front of the whole school? Emma still felt the mortification when her photo with a slave kneeling at her feet appeared at the cork board for everyone to see. The envious, back-stabbing, two-faced friend who had the insolence to pretended nothing happened! It was clear as day that Mathilda wouldn't stop at that. No, of course she wouldn't! She hated Emma too much for being better looking and more popular.... Popular without investing tons of a rich father's money into hair styling and expensive clothes. Emma would look gorgeous even in a potato sack.

Now, after dealing with so many subs over the course of the last year, Emma appeared before Mathilda in even more expensive designer brand clothes than her. Emma recalled with deep satisfaction the first moments when the two had met up that day. Emma flaunted her Dior handbag worth two thousand dollars she bought just to enjoy the perplexed look on Mathilda's face, right under her nose.

Emma could see, when she spotted her in the distance, how her smile froze on her lips for that infinitesimal moment before she adopted her usual, bright, but completely false smile. She knew all the new collections and recognized the Dior bag, the pinnacle of fashion, adorned with embroidered brocade foliage.

"K.O.!" Whispered Emma walking forward to meet her. Mathilda had her old Louis Vuitton handbag that looked like grandma's purse compared to the Emma's red hot handbag that looked as if it had been crafted by angels.

The true battle was going on right behind the surface. Under the sugar-covered words there was a fight raging of popularity, style, wealth and consequence.

"Long time no see my pretty friend. Berlin suits you. It certainly helped you upgrade your style," Mathilda chirped and gave Emma soulful hug and the poisonous kiss.

"Oh wow, your nails are growing so long... I wouldn't wear it myself, but it suits you," Mathilda said, noticing Emma's incredibly long natural nails painted deep red. Emma felt the obvious sting in her voice. Her words were kind, but what it actually meant was: "Your nails make you look like a whore, but I like how classy in comparison I look next to you, so keep them just as they are."
"It is always nice to see a bosom friend, especially one who remains loyal to you even in the most turbulent times," Emma said sweetly.

Emma returned to the present moment. She needed to rein in her sauciness and swallow Mathilda's insolent, hypocritical remarks. Otherwise Mathilda might change her mind and escape her.

"You've been always so good to me. I never will be able to repay you," Emma said and kissed Mathilda on her cheek. Juda's kiss - she thought briefly and recalled the chiaroscuro of Caravaggio's ominous scene on the same subject.

 "Lead the way, I want to see the studio. I've never been to such a place!"

Yet again, Emma didn't fail to capture the tone in Mathilda's voice. It meant: "I despise all the kinksters so much, but I want to observe and study them like some stinky exotic beetles - keeping my distance and snickering about them when they don't look my way."

"Oh, rest assured, I won't keep such a pleasure from you. You are about to meet a magnificent person, a good friend of mine."

Emma took her under the arm and turned left, leaving the main street and walking around few blocks until they arrived to a block of flats. It wasn't Emma's place and the studio they were about to visit wasn't Miguel's. Emma didn't want to bring Mathilda to where she lived. Instead, she used Irina's place.

Emma buzzed the door bell with her forefinger. "My friend is from Poland, she survived the siege of the Warsaw ghetto back in the forties."

Mathilda turned to stare at her. "She did WHAT?"

Before Emma could answer, the deep voice of Irina sounded and the door opened with a click. They ascended several flights of stairs.

"She is from a Jewish family, everyone else perished in the Holocaust."

"She?" Mathilda was confused. Wasn't it an unmistakable male voice she just heard from the speaker?

"...But that's not the important thing, she is first and foremost the most amazing cross-dresser that ever walked the earth."

Mathilda panted and climbed next to Emma the last flight of stairs to the last floor.

"A what?" she said peevishly. She was fed up with Emma using all sorts of unknown terms. She read it as Emma's attempt to gain the upper hand - pretending to be a member of a secret club that she, Mathilda, wasn't part of.
"A transvestite, darling. A transvestite," Emma explained,

purposefully mouthing the words slowly, as if Mathilda was mentally challenged.

An old guy with washed out appearance opened the door for them.

"Irina, darling..." Emma said as she hugged him. Mathilda stared. By the account of Emma she expected a grotesque, glitter covered drag queen. Instead there was very plain, small, rather ugly old man with fish-like eyes, very pointy yellow canines and a balding head, wearing sweatpants and old shirt with threads sticking out of it in every direction.

"Mathilda, this is Irina, a legend among Berlin kinksters..."

The man modestly waved his hand. "I'm no legend, rather a fossil." He stepped aside, cackling, to let them into her apartment. "I'm afraid I don't look representative today, my old illness is plaguing me again."

"Irina suffers from stomach problems ever since experiencing famine during the war," Emma whispered loudly to Mathilda.

"I'm so sorry dear Irina, but I see you always as I saw you first time - the magnificent, striking Lady in the evening gown full of crystal stars."

Emma turned to Mathilda. "..but you can surely tell just by looking at her and her delicate features, that she has all it takes to look stunning with the complete make-up!"
Mathilda hesitantly took old man's offered hand but his look had a weird, unpleasant X-ray quality. She blinked to break the intense eye contact. Mathilda was disturbed by the elderly kinkster as much as Valeria was back at the party where Emma and Irina met for the first time.

"Look there she is in her full glory!" Emma pointed at the wall where a series of framed studio photos shown Irina in her full attire - an evening gown, high heels and exquisite make-up. Mathilda politely showed interest and looked at the photo depicting the most convincing cross-dress she had ever seen. Even though she was so skilled with playing a part, she struggled to find the proper words of praise, facing something she found positively repulsive.

"I'll make a nice drink before your victim arrives," Irina joked.

Mathilda grabbed Emma by the hand. "What on earth is that THING? She... I mean HE of course, looks like a mummy that rolled out of the toilet paper. And this?!" she pointed at the artsy photos - this is really abhorrent! Abomination to nature!"

Emma smiled at Mathilda's lack of tactical thinking. Mathilda clearly thought it was safe to share her disgust with Emma when Irina was out of hearing distance, but in doing so she unintentionally disclosed her profound disgust for everything not vanilla.

Shortly, Irina was back with three blue daiquiris. Mathilda eyed them suspiciously, but Emma took one and sipped it, smacking her lips appreciatively, which appeased her. She also tasted the bright blue drink and the combination of rum, lime juice and cane syrup pleasantly thrilled her taste buds. Mathilda could tell that Irina expected her to say something flattering about her photos.

"I'm sure there is no one else like you," she said eventually with an uncertain smile. It failed to come across as praise, so she tried again. "I mean, wow, what a pretty dress." Her half-hearted attempts to sound courteous didn't fool Irina, who gave Emma a long significant look when Mathilda turned to look at other pictures.

Irina's place was unique, because each and every corner of the large apartment was covered with BDSM photos. Only on one of the walls was a golden frame with white square and a latin 'Horror Vacui' written in the middle in bold Arial Black.

Mathilda knew she wasn't well received, but Irina approached her with her wide smile. "My darling - " she took her hand, "you are very welcome to feel at home here. Let me take you to my den - " she said as she navigated Mathilda to the staircase and propelled her upstairs to the second level of her two-storey apartment. Mathilda looked over her shoulder at Emma.
If she wasn't such a lying, cheating traitor, Emma would be sorry for her. It was written plainly on her face that she actually was very uncomfortable in the present situation. Now she was under the lock with two kinksters she didn't trust at all. Her nosey curiosity suddenly felt like a rather feeble reason to enter the burrow of some old, filthy pervert.

"Don't worry darling, I will wait here for my slave and in the meantime, you enjoy the excursion into the fascinating world of kink," Emma sang out as she turned her back on her, pretending to study the detail of some BDSM themed painting.

When they were out of sight, Emma could hear their steps upstairs. She sat at the table in the kitchen and checked her watch. It was half past two. Her slave was to arrive any moment. She purposefully chose one who would intrigue Mathilda, a very tall guy that would compliment her own, tall figure. Distractedly, she toyed with her glittery bracelet with the BDSM Triskelion. Suddenly, she noticed a piece of folded paper with her name written on it with elegant hand writing. She unfolded it and read:

"Emma, love, there is another daiquiri waiting for you. I'm sure you will find the final result very pleasing. Just leave us undisturbed for twenty minutes and you will be thrilled with the result. I checked everything is in working order, just as you arranged it yesterday."

The corners of Emma's mouth turned slightly down. She struggled with ambivalent emotions. She knew well enough that Irina had more than one kinky identity. Dragging a young, unassuming teenager into her den and leave her alone with Irina was controversial at best... Emma hoped that Irina would stick to the safe - sane - consensual... soon, however, she reconciled her conscience by reminding herself how Mathilda treated her, and that she earned whatever was to happen to her.

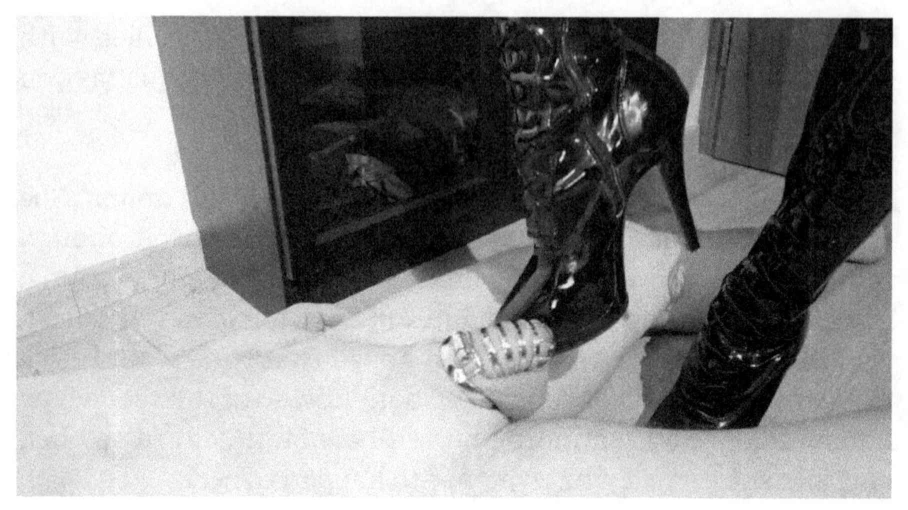

CHAPTER 17

2016

When the doorbell rang, Mistress Emma ventured to open the door. Priscilla, who just went to the kitchen to wash the dishes, stood rooted to the ground. Suddenly the Tom underneath the heavy make up felt faint, standing there in the complete sissy costume. It didn't occur to him, not up to that point, that they might not have compete, undisturbed privacy in the apartment. What if the management of the hotel insisted on going in for some reason?

Priscilla could see through the crack of the door, hoping no one would notice her. But it wasn't a hotel manager. It clearly wasn't anyone having anything to do with the hotel. It was a woman in dark long coat, weirdly out of place in the warm weather like that. She had hair combed back, soothed to the skull so tight it looked like a bathing cap. She had large sunglasses that concealed half her face. When the doors opened, she leaned into the door frame. She was accompanied by two other women in matching coats.

"Hey. Tis Emma?"

"Yes...?" Mistress Emma retorted and judging by the tone of her voice that went up at the end, she was meeting the person for the first time.

"What can I do for you?" she said loudly, authoritatively.

The woman mimicked her tone and it sounded as if the under the surface silent power struggle was going on. The woman didn't smile - another indication of her being very sure of herself and her position.

"Don't pretend you don't know what I'm here for," the strange woman leaned to Emma and whispered. Then she drew back and maintained eye contact with Emma for a few long seconds. Priscilla, standing at the door opened ajar pricked up her ears but couldn't make out what they were saying. The whole situation seemed suspicious. If she read Emma's body language correctly, she wasn't as confident as usual. Was she afraid of something?

"I'm afraid it is not up to me to decide. I'm not the owner...." she turned around and called loudly: "Hannah? Rebecca?"

Shortly, the two women emerged from the living room.

"We are commissioned to take something that belongs to you."

"That remains to be seen," Hannah informed and crossed her

arms in front of herself.

"First show them," was the answer of the stranger.

"Alright. But come in, we don't want the rest of the hotel know of our dealings. Rebecca, will you get them?" Priscilla heard her Mistress' steps approaching - by now she was able to distinguish the sound of each Mistress' steps and Rebecca's shoes made particular clicking sound.

"Charlotte, Priscilla, come out."

Both sissy maids exchanged puzzled looks. "Yes, Mistress."

Priscilla could tell by the perplexed look on Charlotte's face that she was every bit as surprised as she was, and that she had no idea what was going on. They both slowly walked out, looking around themselves carefully. Especially Priscilla felt very vulnerable and uneasy about being seen by someone else other then their close circle of friends.

"Move your ass, bitch," Rebecca said as she propelled Priscilla forward. Charlotte was obediently trotting next to them. Finally, they stood facing the peculiar visitors, awkwardly shuffling their feet and looking intently to the ground.

Rebecca shook hand with the ring leader. "Pleased to meet you."

"Yeah," said the weird woman with poker face. Not a single muscle moved in her face. She took off the large eye glasses and x-rayed the two maids up and down. Priscilla couldn't help but notice the two behind her, who wore the same long coat. They were whispering to each other in hushed voices, covering their mouths with cupped hands.

"Emma, would you mind?"

The woman approached the to two maids, grabbed both of them by the chin and looked them sternly in the eyes. Then she walked around them and scanned them up and down.

"Satisfactory."

"Are you taking them?"

"Yes. We are in a hurry, so let's move. You two, follow."
Priscilla felt like the bottom of her abdomen fell off. He wildly look at his Mistress. What was going on? But Rebecca pretended not to notice Priscilla's agitation.

Mistress Hannah, standing shoulder to shoulder to Hannah, pointed to the door. "You two, go with the Lady. We just sold you for a nice sum. Go and obey your new commander in chief. You are bound to obey her just like you would obey us."

Charlotte and Priscilla looked completely flabbergasted.
"Uh... Mistress?" Charlotte peeped, looking with large, pencil-rimmed eyes, at her Mistress.

"Go now, and show how well I trained you to obey my commands!" Hannah gave her a push to the lower back and Charlotte tripped forward. "Meet your new Owner and show her a proper respect!"

The woman untied the knot on her coat belt and opened it. Now everyone could see that she was wearing a tight, black dress with shiny buckles covering the zipper in the middle.

"Call Me Mistress Camilla," the woman commanded and maid Charlotte dropped on her knees and kissed her shoes. "You will go with me. We have work for you to do."

"N-n-now? Go out of the room? Like this?" Priscilla stuttered. "Don't embarrass me." Rebecca stepped to Priscilla and snapped a leather lead to the D ring on her pink sissy collar and jerked on it, driving Priscilla to her knees. "You will go anywhere Mistress Camilla tells you to go. Mistress Camilla is now your Owner!"

Priscilla hasted to kiss Camilla's shoe, and in the meantime the Lady took the leash from Rebecca. When Priscilla looked up, she tugged on it. Priscilla understood and let herself be guided to her side. She turned and knelt next to Camilla's hip, facing her former Mistress.

"So, now the money." Rebecca said firmly.

Mistress Camilla with few swift gestures made a wireless transfer on her phone and Rebecca checked hers. Priscilla looked at her Mistress with the expression of incredulity and betrayal. Had his wife just sold him? Like really sold him?

"Wow, that was fast. Okay, the deposit was made to my account."

They shook hands and Emma opened the door. "You can go now. You won't have any difficulties, the hotel should be clear. There is a street festival in the city centre. We took precautions."

Priscilla's heart was beating like crazy when she was pulled out of the apartment and the women walked down the stairs. Her brain was a chaos of emotions. What had just happened? Is this a game or did his wife actually sell him to a complete stranger? Who is this Mistress Camilla? Giving Charlotte a sideways look, she looked every bit as surprised as her. This didn't ease her mind - Charlotte was the one experienced with the ways of the Ladies in the Club of the Dominant Wives and yet, she was as taken aback as herself.

They were ushered into the underground garage. There stood

a black pick-up, large enough to use for moving. One of the girls jumped behind the wheel and Mistress Camilla locked the back door with smoked windows open. When she flung the two part doors open, both sissies saw what they didn't expect. They instantly realized that whatever was happening, it was going to be large.

"Take off your shoes," she commanded. "I don't want you to fall on my back."

Priscilla and Charlotte promptly took off their high shoes and carried them to the waiting vehicle.

CHAPTER 18

2016

When Mistress Camilla opened the double door of the big van, Priscilla and Charlotte realized that they were not alone in this. Along the sides of the van were installed seats and in them were another six sissy maids sitting, hunched and looking as comfortable as caged wild animals.

"Welcome to the sissy pick-up, which will transport you to the place of your service," said Mistress Camilla, still in that flat tone. "You are strictly forbidden to talk, or communicate non-verbally. If you break this rule, Miss Martine..." one of the girls gave them a playful wave and twirled a nasty looking twig, "... will take care you will regret it. Take your seat, we have no time to lose."

Priscilla and Charlotte climbed into the van and noticed all sissies were holding their shoes on their laps. They didn't dare to look their way and intently stared to the ground. There was no way to establish eye contact with any of them. One sissy, quite chubby one with angelic curly blonde wig held an extended hand with red marks. She was clearly punished for either talking or trying to make an eye contact with other sissies. There was a smell of sweat in the stuffy space and no way to see out of the van - the windows were covered so that they would have no idea where they were going.

It must have been at least a twenty minutes' drive before the van stopped. Priscilla, who was seated next to the chubby sissy maid, brushed shoulders with it each time the driver stomped on the brake, supposed that they either traveled out of the city or at least to the other side of it. Considering how many times they stopped - presumably at traffic lights or in the crossroads, they were still in the city. Miss Martina was traveling in the back space with them to secure the observance of the ground rules set by Mistress Camilla.

Finally, they could hear the steps outside the van.

"Now, put this on!" Miss Martina distributed among them thick straps of black cloth. "You will use it as a blindfold," she explained.

No one dared to disobey. It clearly didn't occur to them to attempt escape. After all, they got into the tight spot by the command of their Mistresses. They were all conditioned to obey and if their Mistress issued an order to let themselves be dragged into the van and carried devil knows where, they wouldn't dare to resist. It was a Femdom situation through and through.

The doors of the van closed and one by one, each maid,

completely blind and helpless, was assisted out of the van by the two girls. It took a while, but soon they were all standing in a row in what they could only presume was a courtyard somewhere outside. They could feel the fresh air, the last remnants of the sun rays fell on their faces. Their hearing and the sense of touch were becoming sharper, now that they couldn't see what was going on around them.

They all were commanded to extend their hands forward and all of them got fluffy handcuffs snapped onto their wrists. Some kind of rope or a string was stuck through the ring in the middle, binding the two handcuffs together, and his way they formed an orderly queue which was slowly moving forward, navigated by the two girls. They led them indoors. They noticed a change in the air that was suddenly smelling markedly different. Priscilla was guessing that perhaps it was some large, abandoned industrial site. It smelled like it, the floor was cold - clearly a concrete floor - and the echo gave away that there was furniture, no carpets, no textile. They were going on and on, until they walked upstairs, the air getting warmer and they began to smell food.

"Here we are. Now kneel and wait to be summoned."

CHAPTER 19

2008

Irina and Mathilda were still in the playroom of Irina's BDSM studio. Emma fidgeted and distractedly toyed with the bracelet, watching the hand on the BDSM themed wall clock running slowly around and around. Finally, the door bell rang, and interrupted Emma's uncomfortable solitary musings about Mathilda. Why did she care so much about her? Mathilda wouldn't show this much concern for her in a similar situation. Emma used the communicator to let the new visitor in. It was Marcel, the tall, handsome slave, handpicked to 'seduce' Mathilda and make her interested in trying BDSM.

Apparently, Irina took care of that already, eager to help her beloved, cherished Emma. Of course the more Mathilda was exposed to kink, the better the outcome. Marcel, already trained by Emma to respond to wordless commands, immediately took to serve her. She insisted on him keeping his clothes on. She didn't want to repel Mathilda by the unexpected nudity.

On Emma's commands, he mixed another three cocktails. Emma was getting pleasantly relaxed, warmth spreading into her limbs. She took to drinking more while in Berlin and realized that alcohol had that incredible gift to tune down her sometimes slightly too thoughtful and pondering mind. Before she had the first cocktail, she was anxious for her plan to work. Now she just switched into the laid-back approach that was much more conducive to the success of her mission.

Soon, she could hear the heavy door of the playroom open. Hesitant steps were echoing and soon two pair of legs appeared, descending the stairs. Marcel prepared to welcome the 'other Goddess'.

"Emma, dear, your friend's curiosity is insatiable!" Irina called merrily and Mathilda, who slowly walked back into the kitchen, looked dazed and confused. "We had sooo much fun!" Irina chirped happily and downed the prepared cocktail.

Mathilda's drowsily blurry eyes fell on the kneeling man and they instantaneously refocused. Emma knew that Mathilda liked the company of handsome men and she wasted no opportunity to flirt.

"Mathilda, this is Marcel."

"Marcel, welcome Goddess Cordelia," Emma gestured at her to offer her hand for a kiss. Marcel accepted the offered hand and, contrary to the usual rules set by Emma, he looked Mathilda deeply in the eye as he pressed his full, pleasantly shaped mouth on the back of her hand.

"Marcel, today you are going to be my guinea pig! I want to show Mistress Cordelia the wonders of female dominance. I'm sure you are the man for the job. Or rather, the sub for the slave service."

"Cordelia, now that you tried some of the BDSM for yourself, I'm sure you will appreciate the domination of a male as handsome as Marcel."

Mathilda, who turned into Mistress Cordelia - a name she herself came up with, was gaining back her former self. In the events she was surely never to forget, she experienced things she didn't even know existed. Irina's skill in making her do what she wanted and make Mathilda obey, was almost out of this world. She wasn't at all sure what just had happened. She surely never said no, not once, but Irina made her do things she would certainly never ever initiate and under normal circumstances she would certainly refuse. Yet, she found herself in a strange way enjoying what she didn't even realize was a full-blown power exchange with her being the bottom. She enjoyed the powerlessness of her being perched against the wall blindfolded and as Irina was, in a soothing, mellow voice implanting into her head thrilling fantasies, she felt herself getting aroused. Fastening her ankles and wrists to the wheel, she rolled up her skirt. Unbuttoning her blouse and exposed her chest to her gentle fingers she forgot that the person hungrily sucking her breasts actually was a man who could have been her grandfather.

Cordelia felt the power of sexual attraction freely flowing between her and the handsome Marcel. She too drank her third cocktail and her hazy mind soothed down the edges of her self-restraint, already greatly reduced by the brief play with Irina. She delved her fingers into the rich dark locks of the blue-eyed devil.

"So, you will serve me?" she asked, a bit clumsily.

"Yes Mistress, I will do whatever you say. I will adore every inch of your body, I will bear any pain for your sake. Just try me, Mistress."

"Um, okay?" Cordelia said and looked hesitantly at Emma.

"He speaks the truth, he will do all you command."

"Okay, so what if you crawl as a worm?" Cordelia asked, rather indecisively.

"You must say: slave, crawl like a worm!" Corrected Emma and purposefully used exaggerated dominant voice.

Cordelia repeated the formulation in sterner voice and Marcel dropped instantaneously to the ground and began slithering forward, which was ridiculous sight.

Cordelia got into a laughing fit until tears rolled over her cheeks.

"Hilarious!" she exclaimed. "Now - what else can he do?"

"Anything, Mistress Cordelia," Emma said as she winked.

"Aaalright, so, what if you licked my feet?" Marcel didn't hesitate a split second and soon her feet were thoroughly licked and his tongue tickling her between the fingers. She squealed, because it tickled.

"It tickles real bad, how can you stand it?"

"After some time it ceases to tickle, it doesn't tickle me any longer," Emma observed. "Anyway, you see his body, a slave should be naked anyway... But let's go into the playroom, there you can collar him and have him crawl around on a leash," Emma suggested.

Mistress Cordelia led the way upstairs with Marcel crawling on all fours, following her.

"I will be right there!" Emma called and stayed down with Irina. "Did it go... okay?" Emma whispered.

"Darling, why you look so worried? Of course it went okay. I did nothing against her will, if that's a concern. But I was bold enough to drive her to her knees in front of me and have her as submissive as a little lap dog. I was quite surprised how easy it went. Now you do what you do best, and then you've got her. She will never wiggle out of that."

Leaving Irina downstairs, Emma went up to join Cordelia, who, to her utter surprise, didn't need her assistance. She was clearly warming up and seamlessly flew into the opposite role. "And this is how a switch is born..." Emma muttered under her breath.

"Sorry, did you say something?" Cordelia asked.

Marcel had already stripped off his shirt and as his chiseled chin and jawline promised, his body was jacked and nicely toned, his muscle mass just the right amount to look sporty, but not bulky. Cordelia couldn't resist touching him, attracted to the manly form. She was just attaching two small silver bells on a chain to his nipples.

"Nothing, nothing. I was just thinking to myself that you would make for an exquisite Domme!"

"Yeah, I think I'm beginning to enjoy this. Look how obedient he is!" Cordelia giggled.

"Right... he's a good boy! Now, are you curious how he looks underneath? If he looks half as good down there as he looks in the face?

Mathilda was not at all a shy type of girl and even though she was not as experienced as she liked to pretend, she was keen to take another step forward. Emma thought to herself triumphantly, that before the sun went down, she would have Mathilda at her mercy.

"Slave, take off your boxers, I want to see your cock," Cordelia commanded, emphasizing the last word.

Mathilda looked at Emma significantly, observing the effect of her words. What she was saying with her eyes was: "Look at me. Trying this for the first time today and I'm already ruling the game. I would make for a better Domme and make males swoon over me sooner than you!"

Emma could clearly see the lust in her eye when Marcel's swollen, smoothly shaved large cock sprang out from his boxers.

"Wow, what a well-endowed slave Emma, good choice. I think I will keep that one," Cordelia informed. Emma grinned.

"Oh, that breaks my heart, I sort of wanted to keep this one..." Emma called and it was just like pouring fuel into the fire that worked Cordelia up.
Cordelia possessively grabbed Marcel's cock and pumped it. Emma couldn't believe her luck. Her back-stabbing friend was sticking her head right into her own noose. Emma didn't need to do anything, didn't have to persuade her to do anything. She was right there, behaving like a seasoned kinkster, playing her most convincing role ever, probably proud of her acting talent.

Cordelia mightily overplayed her 'Domme persona', but she was not only convincing, she was majestic - perhaps because of the combination of imposing height and dramatic talent. Marcel was so turned on by her rough ways he was aroused as hell, his young penis sticking out at a steep angle.

Emma broadly smiled and comfortably leaned back in a couch, resting her elbow on the high arm rest. Cordelia didn't need help, so she just sipped the daiquiri and enjoyed the performance. She knew that 'Cordelia' was playing her magnificent performance just for her... Another in the row of attempts to bring Emma to her knees. Another try to prove she was better in every respect.

"Now, that's what I call competitive spirit," Emma thought privately and smirked when Cordelia was too busy with exploring Marcel's fit body.

"Do you know he is pretty tolerant of corporal punishments?" Emma casually said.

"Oh! Let's see then!" Cordelia grabbed the nearest cane. She never held a cane in her hand, not once, but she was determined not to get embarrassed.

"Well, well, well..." She whooshed it twice through the air, testing the dynamics of the instrument. "Let's see what your hairy slave ass can take!"

She made the first few strokes, hesitant at first and without much of an impact. But she was learning fast. She didn't want to ask Emma to demonstrate. She was setting one blow after another and Marcel, until her hand gained the certainty. Marcel, who was on the masochistic spectrum, moaned with pleasure.

Just as Emma foretold, before the sun set, Cordelia had her slave eat her pussy right in front of her. She crowned her breathtaking first time Femdom session with strapping a dildo to the slave's mouth and commanded him to fuck her pussy with it. Emma was jubilant, her plan worked much better than she could ever have hoped.

CHAPTER 20

2016

The eight sissy maids stood in pairs behind the closed doors. They were all again wearing their high shoes and stood shoulder to shoulder in a close-knit formation. One of the assistant girls just danced around them with a powder puff, conjuring up clouds around the face of each sissy maid each time she patted one of their faces. When the little green eyed fox tickled Priscilla's nose with the fluffy ball to give her face a matte finish, she grinned nastily. This didn't ease Priscilla's mind a single bit. There could be no doubt as to where they found themselves. Air-handling equipment with silvery tubes under the ceiling, the concrete floors, all referenced the industrial legacy of the place.

From Mistress Camilla, who again took over their supervision, they received the instructions as to their service. She certainly knew how to handle a sissy to get her obedient. She inspected their chastity belts, making sure everything was under control. She checked smoothness of their shave and briefly checked if they were capable of walking on the high heels without falling over. Her stealthy touches, smothering looks, her comments, made Priscilla's head spin.

"I won't have you stink like a male laundry basket at the end of the month," said Mistress Camilla, who took to spraying them with deodorant, just as if they were flies and the spray was an insecticide meant to eradicate them. One of the maids unsuccessfully attempted to suppress a sneeze. The green-eyed foxy girl gave her a contemptuous look.

All were waiting with mixed feelings for the moment when the doors opened. Each and every one of them had jittery knees and they sweated profusely under their elaborate sissy costumes. Behind the closed doors they could hear beats of music, muted laughter and whooshing of whips. Now that they knew why they were summoned and what awaited them, they were very nervous. Perhaps the ignorance was preferable to the mix of anticipation and terror that made them company for the last hour.

Mistress Camilla had a walkie-talkie attached to the belt on her buckled-up dress. The device fizzed and cracked, until another voice sounded: "Camilla, are the maids ready?"

"Yes, the sissies are in place."

"Let them in," said the voice on the other side. Priscilla suddenly realized she knew that voice... It had to be her! No one could sound that eccentric in just the few uttered words but Mistress Cruella.

For a moment Priscilla doubted that her legs would manage to carry her forward - carry her into the midst of the large party of people, who will look at her, laugh at her clumsy ways, her ridiculous costume in which all the manly shapes and edges were mercilessly exposed. Was it the stress that made her senses so much sharper? She was keenly feeling each of the smells - the powder, the deodorant, the sweat, the rubbery flooring, a tinge of mold. Some of the powder got into her mouth and she felt the metallic taste, the sand like structure on her tongue.

Mistress Camilla clapped her hands so loudly, some of the sissies jumped up. Foxy girl flung the door open. "You know what to do!" Camilla shouted loudly enough to make her voice heard over the noise.

"Keep the distance, walk slowly forward, coordinate your step and on the red dot on the floor break the formation, divide in pairs as instructed and start offering the drinks. What are you waiting for, go!"

The first pair, propelled by foxy girl's twig, finally moved. Keeping consistent distance between the pairs, they slowly walked forward, carrying trays with dew covered glasses filled with champagne. The bright party spotlights, roaming at random over the space with black painted walls, blinded Priscilla for a few moments. She blinked in confusion, but her eyes soon adjusted.

What seemed to be a former factory was transformed into a BDSM sanctuary. The floors were covered with red polyurethane rubber for the sake of the high heeled women and men, at the walls stood high-backed chairs, divans with plush cushions. Priscilla realized she was thrown right into a large BDSM party. Ambient red-tinged light, flashing revolving spheres with little mirrors on them and sexy music playing with low, regular beats and the most strikingly sensual mix of sophisticated fetish costumes.

Tom was so humiliated, his cock crammed in the net bodice, swaying on the high heels. To his complete mortification, he noticed several kinksters sending filthy looks and licking lips Pricilla's way. Priscilla, however, was determined not to fail.

"She did it again..." Tom thought, his everyday personality for a fleeting moment overpowering his sissy maid identity. Mistress Rebecca, his devilish, mischievous wife just sold him to serve at a large fetish party. In one fell swoop she managed to break down the last remnants of his male pride. Now he was irretrievably, hopelessly under the spell of female dominance. If he had second thoughts before spring up occasionally on his mind, now it was completely cleared out of his system.

Priscilla almost forgot her instructions when she noticed the amazing Ladies, their naked slaves, dominants with their female slaves and all sorts of other kinksters. The maids, apparently, were the second wave of service crew. Slaves of both sexes, wearing revealing costumes, seemed to be employed for the service a while ago.

Banks' voice suddenly invaded Priscilla's ear, singing Begging for Thread. It weirdly amplified in Priscilla's head, it was curious how of all songs, they just played her favorite one. She knew the words by heart:

Stooped down and out, you got me beggin' for thread
To sew this hole up that you ripped in my head

Stupidly think you had it under control
Strapped down to something that you don't understand

Don't know what you were getting yourself into
You should have known, secretly, I think you knew

The party had just started, people were arriving through the main door, there was laughter and cheers, warm greetings of old friends and cordial introductions of the strangers. Priscilla was parted from her partner in crime, the chubby sissy wearing pink latex uniform that barbarously accentuating her muffin top.

The two assistant girls were still zooming around and issuing additional commands. The foxy one spotted that Priscilla distributed the last of her glasses and received fresh tray, this time serving shrimp appetizers.

"Don't stare, go down the stairs there is a VIP Femdom section."

Priscilla curtsied, carefully, so as to not ruin the culinary masterpieces and headed in the direction foxy girl pointed. Descending carefully, worried she might topple over on her high heels, she heard the unmistakable ringing laughter.

CHAPTER 21

2008

The teenage Emma soaked in a bubble bath, the side of the bath tub was set with tea candles and at her hand was laid assortment of nuts, olives, pastries and a dewy glass of cooled sparkly wine. Miguel had the slave service that day, elated that on that afternoon it was just him and his Goddess. Steam was raising from the water, Emma enjoyed her baths very hot. A soothing music with gentle beats surrounded her and she made the conscious effort to switch off her brain and let herself enjoy the present moment - a heroic endeavor for a person whose mind was at each moment of each day filled to the brim with thoughts. It was a tense week after she received the letter. Now that the danger to herself was averted, she finally could relax.

Miguel, after he finished all his assignments, knelt next to the bathtub. He had to put in a lot of effort into stopping himself from staring at the beautiful Emma, whose sensual body was covered with bubbles. But he could sense her pink nipples whenever she breathed in, her chest heaving. Emma smiled and extended her foot out of the tub. He covered it in kisses and lump of bubbles he brushed off with his chin gave him a white goatee. Emma laughed. She was in good spirits, enough to treat Miguel kindly. Suddenly, she draw her foot back.

"Was that the doorbell?" Emma raised her head from the bathtub pillow.

"I didn't hear it, but I will check, Mistress," was his response.

Four days ago, Emma waved off tipsy Mathilda, overjoyed to see her wide face behind the window of a train, heading back to Köln. She was elated and waved and waved, until the train carrying away her double-faced friend, disappeared around the bend. Then she returned to Irina, who gave her the recordings with Mathilda's wild afternoon. Her BDSM experiments both with Irina and Marcel were all there, in high definition - unmistakably showing Mathilda engaging in behavior that would, to the outside world, look scandalously perverse.

The following day, Emma, who was beyond a shadow of a doubt convinced that it was Mathilda, who sent the letter, posted a package containing a CD with best moments from the recording, accompanied with a pleasant letter describing that from then on, Mathilda would never ever blackmail or denigrate her again, or she would face the consequences.
What would normally be against the grain for Emma, in case of Mathilda felt perfectly justifiable. After all, she was just fighting back. With such powerful material in her hands, Mathilda would

never again do her any harm.

Miguel returned to her.

"Sorry Mistress, but this just arrived."

Emma sat in the bathtub, forgetting entirely about her nudity and sat straight up in the bathtub. It was for the first time Miguel could admire her breasts, perfectly proportionate to the rest of her slender body, yet full and round. He was self-restrained enough not to stare.

"Give it here," she said impatiently and snatched it from his fingers. Right at the moment she heard the door bell, she had a bad premonition. Perhaps the letter arrived the same time of the day as last time, perhaps she subconsciously recognized the plain envelope.

"No... no! No," she shook her head willing it not to contain what she already knew it did. She tore the envelope apart and swiftly flew threw the folded piece of paper with her eyes.

"What is there?" Miguel asked, but for a few moments Emma just stared in front of herself with the expression of shock. "What is in there?" Miguel insisted.

Emma read out: "I'm going to tell at the uni that you are a perverted whore! Or, perhaps you can make me change my mind... Meet me at Hasenheide, I'm sending you coordinates. 5 PM tomorrow. Come alone, or I'm calling into the uni immediately. In case you desired to talk to me, here is my phone number. Nemo"

Emma looked at Miguel. "It wasn't Mathilda after all!"

"I hope you won't go there!" Miguel said.

"Shut it, I can't hear myself think..." Emma's stared somewhere above Miguel's head.

"Okay then, he - I'm sure it is he - will be sorry he was born. I will give him a call, let's see what he's got up his sleeve."

Emma let Miguel to help her out of the bathtub. "Come, Miguel. Get me ready, I'm going out."

CHAPTER 22

2016

Priscilla was descending down, lower and lower, until she arrived to a heavy scarlet drapery covering a door opening. Carrying the tray she pushed the drapes away with her elbow and entered what seemed to be a high-ceiling dungeon with gothic rib vaults. The walls were bare, made of ancient stone, apparently in existence long before the factory that was built on top of it. The room was surprisingly warm and dry, the floors covered with decorative Persian carpets, rugs and sheep skins to keep the Ladies from catching the cold from the stone floor.

The Femdom VIP section was crammed full of women. Priscilla stopped on the threshold, temporarily rendered motionless by the sheer number of the sexy Femdoms in the one single room.

They were in their best clothes, their hairdos, nails and lashes done by professionals, in short they were magnificent in their most glorious form. Almost the whole Club of the Dominant Wives from Berlin was there. Each of the women being waited upon with a kneeling slave at their feet, some of the familiar faces such as Mistresses Emma, Valeria, Hannah, Goddess Eva, Hannah's bald slave, Emma's slave Cunt and a number of Ladies with their slaves he never saw in his life. Andrew's cross and a large wheel already had slaves attached to them and Ladies, probably their Owners, whispering humiliating things - judging by the massive erections they both had.

For some reason Priscilla felt most embarrassed when she was about to serve the women she knew already, but the presence of another at least twenty unknown, dangerously sexy women certainly didn't drive her pulse any lower. When Priscilla entered the room, she immediately noticed Mistress Rebecca sitting at a low table, together with Emma, Cruella and a woman she didn't know.

"Ah, here comes maid Priscilla!" called out Mistress Cruella. "... and with her the much expected shrimps! Rebecca, you have to try these!"

Priscilla approached Cruella and the unknown Lady, a bit rounder around the butt and with sturdy legs sticking out of a revealing mini skirt. Priscilla couldn't help but notice that Mistress Rebecca, who was sitting right next to them, didn't look at her, not even when she grabbed at her tray for the shrimp appetizer. Just as if she was air!

At Rebecca's feet was very young athletic slave that stroked and massaged her feet, his expression closest to religious awe. What was the meaning of this? A pang of jealously coursed through Priscilla like electric current, but she managed to stay in her role and served the shrimps to all the Club members, stealthily measuring his wife, about which he wasn't at all sure if she still was or wasn't his Mistress and Owner.

"Now you serve all the other Ladies and get back into the kitchen for more!" Mistress Cruella commanded, but suddenly she jerked herself, probably realizing that the organizer of the party should be the one to issue commands. "Do you mind, Melissa?"

"Serve yourself, dear," Mistress Melissa smiled. "I've had enough order issuing for one night."

Emma snapped her fingers and pointed her finger at Cruella. "Oh, now I remember - Cruella, I wanted to ask you to tell Rebecca about the case 'Chiara' and she was very interested. I told her about the Femdom weekend and how you were determined to get a revenge. Would you tell her more about how it turned out?"

"Gladly! Always happy to entertain my friends, as long as - " she looked at Melissa - "as long as Melissa is fine with that."

Melissa didn't hear her, she was just turned to the neighboring table, talking to someone else.

Emma fished the alcohol infused strawberry from her tall champagne glass with her long finger nail and popped it into her mouth, munching on it happily. "Anyway, I lent Rebecca my diary, if you asked her where she stopped reading you might save a lot of breath on repeating what she already knows."

Cruella looked at Rebecca, clearly surprised with Emma's level of trust. Rebecca felt her look and realized Cruella was weighing her character. It was a bit insulting, but she wasn't in the Club as long as the other members. She realized that she would have to convince Cruella just as she convinced Emma that she is a completely reliable and honest person.

"Emma was so kind to let me into her privacy, I'm eternally grateful to her for it, because it has immense educational value for me as a new Domme."

Cruella, who wasn't by nature a suspicious sort of person, seemed satisfied. "I see, well, whomever Emma trusts with her own diaries, I can also tell the story of Chiara. What do you think Melissa?"

Rebecca looked at her, a bit puzzled, for she again addressed a woman, who had nothing to do with it. But Melissa was a hostess after all, she certainly had the authority to decide if it is time for a story or if she has, for instance, a Femdom game up her sleeve. This time Melissa heard the question and expressed no objections.

"I've got to the point when you met in café Perdu and you disclosed to Emma that you have a better plan to deal with Chiara. I mean that you decided against good old revenge. As you put it - you didn't want to mess up your karma."

"Yeah, back than I realized that it would probably blow up in my own face, if I decided to punish Chiara. I sensed - no, I knew, that she wasn't beyond salvation just yet. The changes to her character were not permanent. Me and other Ladies of my acquaintance put our heads together and we came up with a plan. Hannah and Emma was part of it, as well as their slaves."

"I guess I already know where this is heading..."

"If Emma told you about Marcus, Chiara's husband, I would be surprised if you didn't."

"Yeah, Emma described in great detail what she learned about him from you, how he was essentially exploiting Chiara and making her do things she otherwise wouldn't."

"Quite right! My reasoning was that if we managed to make Chiara see through his manipulative, gass-lighting ways, she might break free from him and, with a bit of help from her friends, find her long lost equilibrium. I was sure she hadn't forgotten what being a Dominant Lady actually means. To the outside world she still meticulously stuck to the outward signs of Femdom, but she was as sub as it gets."

Mistress Melissa cleared her throat. "Okay, I take that back, Chiara wasn't a sub, she was just a bit confused. Will you let me tell the story, or would you like to tell it yourself?" Cruella said to Melissa in a merry tone.
"No, sorry to interrupt, I'd rather not."

"Well, back then I knew from my other Domme friends, that Marcus was cheating on Chiara. I heard that directly from one of the Ladies, with whom he had been unfaithful. And by unfaithful I don't mean just D/s or Femdom scenes, but regular sex. He was the sort of insatiably erotomaniac of a man that never ceases to pursue the next woman he meets. Add to it an obsession with the weirdest things and he wasn't the sort of partner you would want for yourself."

Emma weighed in. "Perhaps you recall, Rebecca, what I told you about Marcus' fantasies."

"Yeah, I do. It stuck in my mind, for it seems a bit over the top even for me. He wanted to be forced to have sex with gays in a Berlin park forest."

"Right. Chiara, even though she usually strived to fulfill each and all Marcus' fantasies, was totally against it."

Hannah said: "Clearly! Who would approve for your husband to have unprotected sex with gay guys, who enjoy hanging around and fucking everything that goes by...?"

"Right, so me, Emma and Hannah agreed to do a number on him. He was regularly seeking new dates and new exciting experiences online. We got Mistress Hannah to establish a connection with him."

Hannah said: "I made him believe that I would fulfill his fantasy and have him fuck the gay guys in the forest, just as he wanted."

"Wow, that sounds crazy," Rebecca stared. "And also a bit dangerous."

"It was crazy. If I didn't have my slave there to have my back the whole time, I would probably have been quite scared. But we were determined to pull it off. I met Marcus in the park. I had never seen him before so I was quite surprised that he didn't fall even a little bit short of his reputation. He was incredibly weird and sleazy. I had goosebumps when he began to remove his clothes in front of me. Luckily, the whole thing went even better than any of us expected. Not only was he eager to do the hook up, but he made the most convincing show to the camera, held by my slave in a shrub nearby. He professed undying love and obedience to me. He expressively claimed he would adore and admire no other woman. You can imagine how heartbroken Chiara would be, when she learned just how easily her slave husband went around swearing his loyalty to other women."

Mistress Melissa said "It would take a woman either completely dumb or desperate to keep her illusions of the man after that..."

"I'm glad you think so, Melissa," Hannah said significantly. "So, as we walked in the direction of the place where the gay guys met, I had him explain to me the details of his fantasy. He, of course, was very specific about how he wished it to happen. When I had all of that on camera, I pretended a change of heart and I just backed away. He was very disappointed and didn't even offer to accompany me on my way back to the car. I assume he was resolved to stick to the plan anyway."

"Oh, I dare say that Chiara must have been destroyed by learning what scumbag she married..." Rebecca said a bit sadly.

"I was indeed," said Mistress Melissa.

Rebecca looked at her with her eyes wide open. "Excuse me?"

"I was destroyed, yes," Melissa said emphatically.

Rebecca looked from Emma to Hannah, from Hannah to Cruella and back again.

"Well, it is true, Mistress Melissa used to be Chiara. She just change her name - to cut herself from everything that had something to do with Marcus." Emma said.

"Right, I wanted to leave that part of my life behind," she explained. "I even moved out of Berlin, taking permanent residence here in Dresden. I dropped my professional Femdom career and returned to what I used to do before and work again in real estate."

"Oh, so it worked then? The strategy Ladies came up with to convince you that Marcus was just using you?" Rebecca wondered.

"It did work, indeed. At that very moment I hated them for ruining my marriage. It was very hard at that point, but I'm better off without Marcus. He was treating me horribly. I didn't realize at the time! I have to give credit to the Ladies here that they saved me from the tentacles of the monstrous man. Of course at first I was trying to defend him, but Cruella made me face the evidence that was overwhelming. Earth shattering. And first and foremost, undeniable! I had my suspicions before, but I tried to shun it. Every time a new piece of evidence emerged, I turned a blind eye to it. But after I saw the recording I was forced to face the truth. Not only was he cheating on me most days of the week but he professed undying love to each and every one of the women he met. And he wasted no opportunity to denigrate me, slight me and laugh at me for my loyalty and unyielding trust. His behavior truly was outrageous. I fail to see how I could be so infatuated with him. He was playing me, aiming at my softest spots, sticking needles into the most sensitive corners of my soul, in short he was as toxic a partner as you can possibly think of."

"But you got over it, judging from this marvelous party, you are back in the game!" Rebecca smiled.

"Yes, first and foremost I have to thank Cruella, the great psychologist, who realized that the parasite had to be removed from my brain. She would make for a great exorcist! What's more, at the first opportunity, she hurled my way my present partner, my slave Basil."

Rebecca finally noticed the slave at Melissa's feet.

"If it hadn't been for Cruella, I'm not sure what would happen to me. Now I'm living blissfully happy life and enjoy true Femdom with my sweet Basil."

"Melissa regrets all that passed between us and ever since she ditched Marcus, she's been one of the best friends I've got," Emma said. "Now, we have two cool Clubs, the Dominant Wives Club in Berlin, and Mistress Melissa Femdom Club here in Dresden. That way we are never short of great parties!"

"I hope, Rebecca, that I will see more of you, now that I bought your servant."

Rebecca looked sideways at Priscilla, who albeit was zooming around with her tray, was listening intently.
"Right, I also appreciate the sum. She is, after all, still rather inexperienced, so it was pretty good offer."

"Well, Mistress Camilla saw potential in her the very first moment, she has quite an eye. Priscilla is quite the looker! You'd be surprised how difficult it is to get a sissy that is not overbearingly clumsy, fat or way too tall to look good in the sissy costume."

Priscilla froze in an awkward position, suddenly aware they were talking about her. So Rebecca did sell her after all. Was it even possible? They were married after all... But in the universe where women rule, Priscilla knew that everything is possible.

Dear reader!

Did you enjoy this book?

If you did, you will please me very much if you share your thoughts in a favourable REVIEW on Amazon store. (When you are there, you may pre-order volume 3 of this series!)

Your contribution will help me realize my dream of becoming successful writer. Help me today to make my dream come true!

Also be sure not to miss the opportunity to volunteer as a beta reader for my upcoming books. If you want to help editing or proofreading my books, get in touch on my website.

Your PhDomme Emma,

the founder of the University of Slavery and Servitude

TEASER FOR VOLUME III

The e-book version of the final installment is already available for pre-order!

Don't miss the final volume of the story based on the real life of Mistress Emma, the founder of the University of Slavery and Servitude, educator and successful Femdom erotica writer.

The third and last volume of the "My Femdom Marriage" series is not only an engaging read, it is also a riveting probe into real world Femdom for all fans of female dominance, and those who desire in the bottom of their heart to find their own Femdom. More than fifteen years of experience with BDSM and D/s relationships gives Emma's style inner truthfulness and her storytelling gift adds suspense, unexpected twists and vivid characters.

In the last installment you will again follow the adventures of the Ladies of the Dominant Wives' Club, who will further unravel the fascinating life of women who enslaved their husbands and turned them into chaste, obedient and humiliated servants who fulfill their every need.

In the previous volume Mistress Rebecca, always eager to live new Femdom experiences, sold her husband Tom to the Dresden

Femdom Club to serve as a sissy maid. Priscilla, who was trained for a house maid by the professional Mistress Hannah, was left wondering what will happen to her. Did her Mistress really sell her, or is it just another of her unorthodox ways of making her husband push his boundaries?

Mistress Emma removed the harmful influence of Mathilda from her life, but to her surprise, she wasn't the one who sent her the mysterious blackmail letters. Who decided to make her life hell and ruin her prospects of traveling to the UK to study?

The summer arrived and the Ladies of the Club decide to spend their vacation on a yacht in the Mediterranean. Get thrilled by the sexy story and let yourself be drawn into the suspenseful narration that makes you turn pages until you devour the whole book!

The e-book version of the final installment is already available for pre-order!

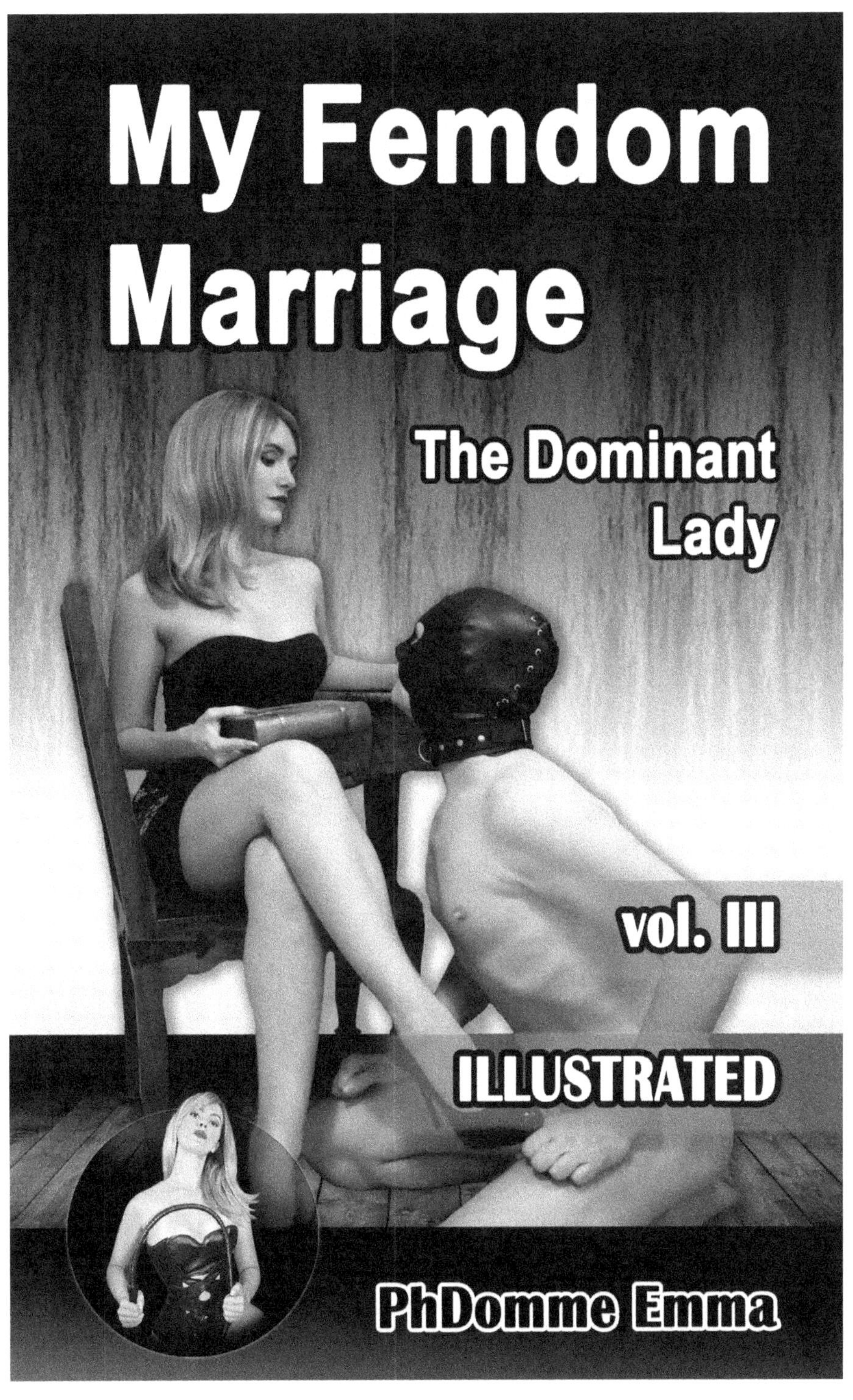

My Femdom Marriage
Marriage
The Dominant Lady
vol. III
ILLUSTRATED
PhDomme Emma

ABOUT THE AUTHOR

Phdomme Emma

A natural Dominant Lady in whom you can find the unique combination of gorgeous looks and sharp mind. PhDomme Emma is a founder of the University of Slavery and Servitude, an educational and dating platform for Dominant Ladies and submissive men who love them.

The Femdom lifestyle was ever since Emma's early youth the only way of life imaginable. Born into comfort and raised as a Princess, she soon learned how to command men. Becoming briefly a professional Dominatrix in her eighteenth year, she gained invaluable experience with BDSM. However she dropped professional Femdom career in favour of truly independent adventures and became a teacher and instructress for those, who still struggle to find the Mistress of their dreams.

Emma keeps unraveling the endless universe of Femdom by interacting with those, who are willing to fully sacrifice their heart, body and soul to the selfless service and adoration of

Dominant Women. She owns her permanently chaste 24/7 slave for 13 years and keeps exploring the fascinating world of Female Dominance and male submission with men, women and couples. Her wild and adventurous youth followed by serious life challenges moulded her into the confident, strong, yet emphatic and balanced personality whose raison d'être is to help others achieve the happiness she herself was so lucky to attain. She have met dozens of D/s couples, Dominant women and submissive men, whom she helps to make sense of the often complex world of lifestyle Femdom relationships.

In her educational courses and in her tutorials Emma teaches submissive men the skills to impress the Dominant Lady they always dreamed of and to establish a mutually satisfying D/s relationships. PhDomme Emma's ambition is to reach especially to those submissives, who know in the bottom of their heart, their place is at the feet of a Dominant Lady, but who lack the opportunity and guidance of a wise teacher to achieve their potential. Emma is convinced that every worthy submissive should find his happiness in the service to a Dominant Lady. For this reason her books will always be so cheap that positively anyone can afford them.

In her novels of which the Femdom Syndicate Trilogy is the first instance, she lets her kinky fantasy soar. Her stories are in many cases based on real life situations of her adventurous BDSM life which gets better and better every day. Peek through the keyhole into the bedroom of a sexy Dominatrix!

Follow her Femdom Adventures on Twitter, BDSMlr, Tumblr and Fetlife.

Also don't forget to check Her blog!

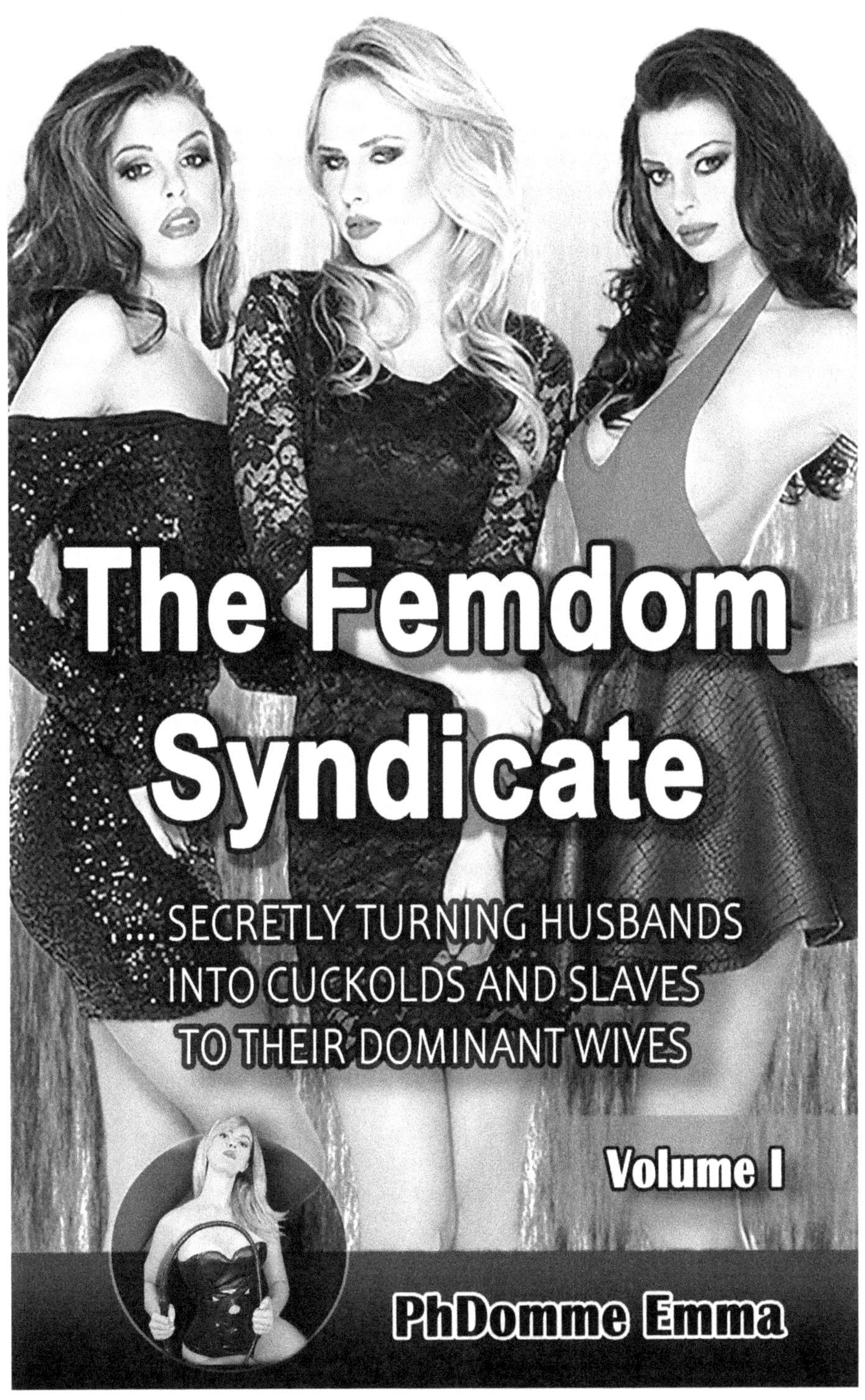

The Femdom Syndicate
... SECRETLY TURNING HUSBANDS INTO CUCKOLDS AND SLAVES TO THEIR DOMINANT WIVES
Volume I
PhDomme Emma

BOOKS BY THIS AUTHOR

The Femdom Syndicate Trilogy

Read PhDomme Emma's bestselling trilogy! Are you ready to enter a world of predatory Dommes, who turn husbands into obedient slaves to their wives?

On the outside, Amy and Michael may seem like an ordinary married couple. Amy owns a little art gallery in New York. Michael, her loving husband, is secretly harbouring submissive feelings toward dominant women. His persistent fantasies of Femdom cuckold adventures were as yet never fulfilled. Amy is, like a proper wife, initially repelled by the idea of cheating on her husband.

But when both embark on a journey to Berlin, they meet a handsome stranger, who brings Amy to question her resistance to an open marriage. She has no idea there is already an elaborate scheme in place that will change both her and Michael's lives forever.

After Amy's chance encounter with a gorgeous guy on the plane, and an offer from his good friend Emma to stay at Her beautiful country mansion, things heat up quickly for the vacationing couple.

Before they realize what is happening, they find themselves being drawn into a world of Femdom hierarchy and control, from which there seems to be no escape. They are led deeper and deeper into an erotically charged web of irresistible seduction and control.

Amy's eyes are opened to a world of sexual experiences she never thought possible, too distracted to realize that her husband has fallen into the hands of a very dangerous Dominatrix.

The Adventures Of A Young Dominatrix

Meet Cristine, a confident and sexy 18-year old girl who has a knack for wrapping men around her finger. Follow her adventures through this femdom suspense trilogy with an engaging plot that keeps you on your toes, while the steamy scenes of female dominance will keep you up at night!

Cristine was raised in the Christian spirit by a foster family and educated at a stern Catholic school. Much to the disappointment of her religious parents, she is far too attractive and clever not to notice the power her beauty provides over men and boys. She doesn't miss a single opportunity to make submissive males crawl at her feet and do her bidding!

Her parents, scandalized by her naturally dominant inclinations, sign her up for a Catholic summer camp in a last ditch attempt to get her on the right path before she goes off to college. Things heat up quickly when Cristine uncovers a horrible secret, kept under wraps by the administration at her high school.

Before she can even think about leaving for Catholic camp or college, she must exact her own brand of justice and expose her school's scandalous secret. Her stunning act of bravery makes the national news, much to the horror of her family.

Unfortunately, it seems that no good deed can go unpunished and Cristine finds herself pursued by a dangerous psychopath, and then trapped by a cult-like group of religious zealots at an old English Abbey.

Her attempts to escape the hell of their religious indoctrinations and corporal punishments find Cristine involved in many sexy and kinky encounters with submissive males and lesbian females, daring escapes and shocking revelations. Cristine starts to learn the fascinating truth of her family and she is introduced into the sensual world of femdom that she never dreamed could have existed. Join Cristine on her adventure!

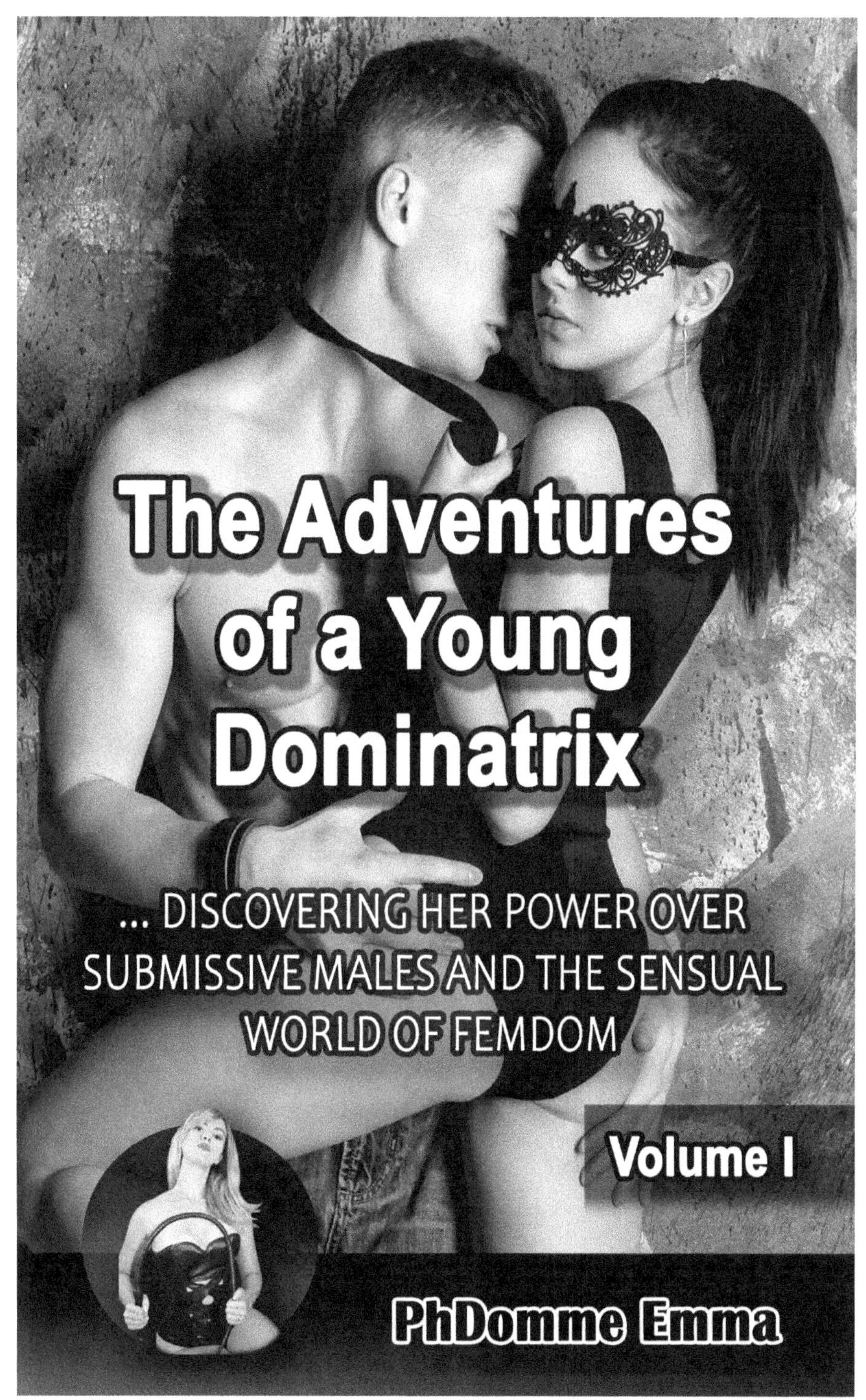

The Adventures
of a Young
Dominatrix
... DISCOVERING HER POWER OVER
SUBMISSIVE MALES AND THE SENSUAL
WORLD OF FEMDOM
Volume I
PhDomme Emma